CLAYTON

The Wildflower Series 1

BY RACHELLE MILLS

CLAYTON

Limitless Publishing, LLC
Kailua, HI 96734
www.limitlesspublishing.com

Formatting: Limitless Publishing

ISBN-13: 978-1-64034-487-7
ISBN-10: 1-64034-487-X

Dedication

For the Wildflowers, thank you for the belief that I am more than who I thought I was. The start of this book was the seeds being planted and nurtured and turning into a community about us that is flourishing and blooming. Thank you for inspiring me, Wildflowers.

CHAPTER 1

A Choice

I wrap my hands around the wooden pole, and they're latched with a delicate silver chain that I have no hope of breaking.

The Alpha has delivered justice for my attack of another pack member.

The whole pack has gathered to watch, my mother's eyes weeping tears for me, my father's head hung in shame. I try looking at my mate, but he just holds my competition in his arms, rubbing her back in comfort, her face still bruised and swollen from the beating I gave her. She's lucky someone pulled me off or else I think I could have ended her life with my leap into insanity.

The Alpha, my mate's father, is looking around to all the pack members while the whip hangs lightly in his hand, as if it doesn't hold a heavy weight. The fabric of my shirt is cut down the back, exposing skin that is about to be scarred with the cruel touch of the lash.

"I called you all here today to witness Rya's punishment. She has attacked another member of this pack without provocation." He's speaking the truth for the wind to bring to the ears of all those listening. I did attack her, an escalation of words turning into violence between two females wanting the same male.

Except I am his mate, and she is his everything.

I went to him as soon as I shifted, knowing who he was to me. She was there; she has always been there since they could walk. He must have known I was his even before I shifted, yet he continued on with her. I begged him, pleaded with him to just give me a chance, making a scene for all to witness. He told me to *go, leave.* That she might not be his true mate, but she is the one he wants, regardless of what the moon thinks.

She stood there, not saying anything, as I made a fool out of myself, her perfect face staying stoic the entire time as he dealt with me, a crazy she-wolf fighting for what she thought was hers.

In a moment of absolute rage, I took that step into insanity, with the intent to kill her, my wolf wanting to eliminate the competition. And I, I decided to embrace the darkness my nature provided. He stopped me. He protected his chosen female from his mate's wrath.

The first stroke of the whip tastes my back, greedily devouring my pristine flesh. I don't look away from my mate, his hand crushing hers. I notice how white her fingertips look as they are deprived of blood. I try to be brave, gritting my jaw against the pain. The next stroke takes me off-

2

guard, and I cry out in agony. A young juvenile female is no match against the justice the whip provides. Even full-grown males beg and plead for mercy given enough hits from the lash.

Embedding its lethal kiss into my skin, I will always wear my shame for others to see. Another sickening crack screams through the air, cutting another furrowed groove deep into the skin. Blood splatters on the ground, forming a carpet of red.

I can no longer keep his eyes; my head bows, salt tears trail off cheeks, falling to the ground, mixing with my blood. It's as if I'm the other jealous female, and she's his true mate. That's how I am being treated like: the psycho crazy female.

Black shoes come into my line of sight. "Rya, you know why I'm doing this?"

Nodding my head yes to the Alpha, I respond quietly, "I understand."

"What do you understand, Rya?"

I'm crying now with what I have to say. "I tried to kill another pack member."

"That's right. You can't go around trying to kill another female because your mate does not want you." My head hangs even lower, my body shaking from my sobs.

"You have to respect choice, Rya; he doesn't choose you. He chooses her. You need to respect this and accept this." His voice is very stern, authority ringing out for everyone to hear.

"Do you understand this, Rya, that he doesn't want you?"

My shoulders are shaking with the truth I am hearing. "Yes, I understand."

"You're to leave them alone, you cannot speak to them unless spoken to, and you cannot follow him around anymore—no contact. Do you understand?"

"I do."

"You have three more lashes. From now on, you are to eat last. You will be at the back of the pack until I tell you otherwise. Do you understand?" The Alpha sounds pained to say this, but it is the usual punishment that is doled out for misbehaving she-wolves who can't get over their lovers. Except usually, these she-wolves are replaced by mates, not mates who are rejected.

"I understand." I grip my hands together, and he makes the whip sing through the air, raining down hard and fast, robbing me of breath. The second strike has sounded, and I scream between gritted teeth. The final strike of the silver lash is meant to be remembered. It drops me to my knees in front of my pack, my parents, and him—my mate. The pain is so great, yet it doesn't compare to the way my heart has just been torn away. The healer is there instantly, taking the binding from my wrists. Looking up, I see Clayton kissing Kennedy's forehead, turning their backs on me, walking away hand in hand.

I can't breathe.

My legs refuse to lift my weight. Instead, I stay kneeling with my shoulder against the blood-stained pole for support.

"Let's get you up." The kindness the healer shows me is more than I deserve.

"Just leave me here," I whisper. My mother comes over to me, crying. That also hurts my soul, the shame she has to carry, my family has to carry, from my dance with insanity. Just a second without thinking has led me to this moment. Never again will I not think before I act. A cooling cloth is pressed onto my back. Smelling of medicine, it numbs the pain slowly.

"I'm sorry, Mother." Still, my voice is shaky with the need to cry. My father's back is to me; he leaves without another word.

"Let's get you home." Wrapping an arm around my body, the healer helps me to a standing position. The effort makes sweat roll off my forehead. The healer takes my other side, and I'm somewhat dragged, carried to my home. I lay face down on the bed, and the ointment is spread over the ruined flesh, more bandages applied. My mother is given directions from the healer on how to treat me. A cup is pressed against my lips, and the tart liquid makes my nose scrunch up.

"It's so you can sleep." I finish the concoction before being left alone in my room to think about my actions.

It takes three days before I don't need help getting out of bed to go to the bathroom. Three more days for me to be able to walk on my own. Another two more days to go back to school.

Walking into the cafeteria, I have to endure the sight of them together. I have two more years left; they graduate in the spring. At least I don't have long till I no longer have to see them every day.

My friends have turned their backs on me, pretending I'm not standing there, hoping they make room for me to sit with them.

"I'm sorry, Rya, but all the spots are taken. No room for you anymore." I don't say anything back to Cora. It's no use. Turning away, I take my lunch outside and sit underneath one of the maple trees. The leaves are just starting to unfurl, providing a small amount of shade from the sun. Being alone, shunned now from the group I grew up with, has me silently nibbling my sandwich as it catches my tears.

I'm picked last for group projects; gym class has me the odd-man-out. The teachers don't say anything; I'm not sure they even notice the shift in status. The humans around us just think I'm fighting with my group of friends.

No one is physically violent with me. They just treat me as if I don't exist. Like I have no feelings. The worst are the pack gatherings. Most of the time I just refuse to go, holing up inside my room, a grey cloud following me wherever I go.

I have to watch as he makes a plate for himself and her. Always he's providing her with food for the pack to see. As the last to eat, only the unwanted items are left for me. Usually, I go without. Sitting at the back by myself, unable to even eat with my own family, I'm in my own private purgatory that I endure quietly without complaint. Sometimes, on very rare occasions, I can feel his eyes on me. But, just as fast as I feel them, they're gone. I try not to look at him anymore for fear he will be able to feel my gaze as well.

Two years I endure this. It's a lonely, miserable life. It's funny how you grow and mature and the body people see looks healthy and young, except for me it's just a shell covering my emptiness.

I've applied for a transfer out of my pack, and the Alpha has granted my wishes, with the understanding that I am to come back when needed. My marks have been above average, and I've been accepted to apprentice as a midwife underneath the guidance of a much-esteemed female. The healer helped me with my application, I was interviewed, and my grades were looked at. My commitment level was assessed; they just don't want anyone who will drop their training once they meet their mate. She was made aware of my situation, accepting me instantly. A sad smile tugged at her eyes as she welcomed me into her home with a hug.

For the first time in two years, I have a smile that reaches my eyes with what my future might be.

CHAPTER 2

Coming Home

Insomnia is a great company to grief. Like two old friends unable to part, they mingle with each other, never letting the other go completely.

"Couldn't sleep." My mentor is sitting by the fireplace that holds no fire, with a cup of tea in her hand, looking at me with caring eyes.

"No, I couldn't sleep. Big day today." I can't even disguise my sadness.

"Are you all packed up? Do you have everything?" Her voice cracks as well. Mentor and student at first, but once my training was completed, we became good friends.

"Rya, it's going to be okay. You're going to be okay." I wish I could believe that.

"It's going to be okay." I say it out loud over and over again, trying to fool myself.

"I just need to thank you for everything you've done for me. I appreciate all your teaching, but especially your kindness when I needed it the most." Standing up, she walks toward me, opening up her arms so I am pressed against her ample chest, cheeks rubbing together.

"You're going to be great, my best student I have ever had the privilege to teach. You're a beautiful female inside and out. Remember that." She wipes away my tears as I try to control my breathing like she taught me.

"I need to go. It's a long drive. Thank you again." Walking out of the house we shared for the last four years is so hard. This has been my fantasy land, protecting me from a life I am not forced to go back to.

In the rearview mirror, I see her waving in the open doorway. I give a little wave as I pull out. I start to drive toward what gives me my nightmares at night.

Pulling up to the pack house, I need to sit in the car to gather my wits. I need to check in, get the keys to my new home. The Luna felt it's better if I just take over the old midwife's house, seeing as it's empty now.

The day the phone rang was like any other day for me, a birth in the early morning hours that went well for both mother and pup. I was just coming out of the shower when I picked up the phone. It was the Alpha. I almost dropped the phone.

You're needed back here. That's all he said to me before the Luna took over the conversation, telling me the midwife has passed back to the moon. How I need to *come home.* I knew this was inevitable. I just thought I would have more time. I haven't seen my father in four years. My mother and sisters have visited once, but there was an awkwardness to us that never existed before. My mother wanted to visit me more, but I just pretended that I was too busy, that I had lots of work, that it was impossible for me to get away.

As soon as I open the door, his scent hits me hard, so hard that I need to go back inside my car and close the door. I hold the steering wheel, gripping it so tightly my knuckles are white. I wasn't prepared for it. I haven't even seen him yet, and I'm reduced to immobility. I stay like this for a few minutes, or ten, I'm not sure. I try to give myself a talking to, scolding my own reactions to something that is so natural like breathing.

How do you tell yourself not to *breathe*?

Unclenching one hand, then the other, I wipe sweaty palms on my shorts. The car is starting to heat up with the sun's hot rays beating down on the metal. Big breath in, I open the door, making my shaky legs take me toward the front door. I knock, waiting for it to open. The Luna greets me with a smile on her face. I smile a decaying smile back.

"Look at you, Rya." She lets her eyes roll over my body. "You have grown into a beautiful female." She presses her cheek against mine in welcoming. I'm not the small juvenile I once was. I'm a full-grown female wolf.

"Your eyes, Rya, stunning." Glacier blue, my greatest asset as I was told once. Almost the color of a blue moon that only comes around every few years.

"Thank you." His scent has tentacles that wrap around my body, seducing me with something that I sometimes dream about. It's extremely hard to concentrate on anything she tells me. Her mouth is moving, smiling. I just nod my head, pretending she holds my eyes.

She walks me inside slightly; her office is the first door to the right. I sit in the chair across from her, and she pushes an envelope toward me.

"Keys. One set is to the house, and the second set is to the clinic. You'll be working alongside the doctor until he feels you're okay to be on your own." She has her hands folded on top of her desk.

"Rya, I'm sorry it has to be this way." I look into her eyes; she appears sad, but looking around her office, I see pictures of her immediate family, all smiles for the camera. She's not sorry. I can't look at him for too long. My eyes will start to water.

"Thank you, Luna Catherine, for the opportunity to serve the pack." I keep it extremely formal, back straight in my chair, hands on my lap, head bowed in submission.

The office door opens. "Cathy, look at these. Aren't they so cute?" Kennedy, by the first glimpse of her...the full-grown female, standing in the open doorway, her reddish hair with glints of copper and rust from the sun shining on her through the open blinds. Her freckles are just a shade darker than her suntanned skin. Eyes are brown, not a good feature. Her neck holds the red angry marks of a male who claims a female who isn't *his*. That, at least, gives me some satisfaction...that she cannot hold his mark no matter how much he tries. The moon doesn't allow impostors to hold claims from another. It must cause her pain to have his mark, the

11

moon's punishment. Looking away at my feet, I keep my head bowed, not saying a word.

"Oh, I didn't know you had company, Cathy." Lie one. Clasping my hands more firmly together, I try to keep the fur that wants to raise along the ridge of my spine down.

"Rya?" The way she says my name, it's like she's surprised to see me. Lie two. She had to have known I was coming today.

"Hello, Kennedy." I've practiced the voice in front of the mirror so many times, it comes out naturally, devoid of any emotion. It's held flat in the air. I don't make eye contact; it's better for me this way. I keep my head bowed down to the future Luna of the pack in a show of respect that is expected of me.

"Hello, Rya." Her voice cannot hold her emotions in. It's slightly shaky, like the way my body feels at the moment. She smells just like him. Bile wants to rise up. I force it down.

Standing, I bow slightly to the both of them.

"Thank you, Luna Catherine; I should be going." Taking the envelope from the table, I walk out, not breathing in until I'm outside.

The alpha is leaning on the driver's side door, waiting for me. I don't focus on what's in front of me; the sensation of being watched has the hair on the back of my neck raising. Heat, hot burning sensual fire from the spot that holds his attention, my back blazing with warmth...his sight moving down my back, over my ass, caressing my legs, back up my body...until I feel it no more. It reminds me of having a suntan, my skin keeping all the warmth I felt from his eyes.

"Rya, it's good to see you."

"Thank you, Alpha. It's good to be home." Monotone. That's how I keep it. No need to show inflection. I can be who they want me to be. I can be nothing but a ghost floating on the outskirts of the pack. This is not the life I pictured for myself so long ago, while still a small pup being rocked to sleep by my mom.

"We won't have any trouble, right, Rya?" He waits for my reply. He doesn't have to wait long. I reply instantly without a second thought.

"No, Alpha, no trouble. I've learned my lesson. I respect his choice." I keep my head bowed, tail tucked under.

It's as if I'm the mistress, hell-bent on destroying their made-up bond. The only consolation is that they can't breed; only true mates are blessed with the moon's gift of pups.

"Rya, I'm sorry about all this. I don't understand his choice, but it's his to make, no matter how wrong it is. Maybe one day—"

"It's all right. I really don't want to talk about it. What is done is done. I've moved on." Still not meeting the Alpha's eyes, I open my door, getting in before more can be said.

I know exactly where I'm going as I pull away from the pack house to the little cottage on the curve of the lake. Not far away from the hustle and bustle of the pack house, but far enough to give me the privacy I crave.

The key to the house is a perfect fit, small and unassuming. I turn the knob, and it's as if I stepped back one hundred years in time. Exposed wooden beams with a sloping ceiling...very charming, except it smells of an old female wolf.

I open a window, and the warm wind blows in the scent of deep summer, the breeze moving my long hair, tickling my skin. The walls must be thick to keep the temperature cool. The door opens up to the living room. Flagstone for flooring is cool underneath my feet once my sandals are kicked off.

I feel like an explorer would, taking in all the nooks and crannies of the place, my place now. Empty jars line the open cupboards of the kitchen; she must have loved to can things. Recipe books litter the bookcase, along with her own handwritten books that midwives keep.

The place is clean and tidy. I notice there is no television, only books that probably took up the majority of her nighttime entertainment. The furniture is not overcrowding. A comfy couch, an end table, and a La-Z-Boy chair. It's the kitchen table that catches my eye. Long and slick, cut from the trunk of a tree that has been sanded and stained. It takes up most of the room, so thick probably many male wolves were used to move it in here. Running my hand along the entire surface, it's smooth against my fingertips. I can picture the late night parties I could hold here if things were different.

Starting to work, opening up all the windows, I air it out so it will start to smell of me. Like I belong here now. An old stove sits in the corner of the room, galvanized steel, made a century ago that needs to be fed with wood to cook on. I welcome the challenge; my mentor taught me on her own stove, so this shouldn't be much of a problem.

Is this what it's like to be a spinster wolf at twenty-two? All I need are the cats to come around and make my home theirs. I open up the fridge. Nothing is in there. Opening up the cupboards, I find they are barren. I have to do a giant grocery trip to stock everything I need.

The bed is in a tiny room, and the mattress has the plastic still on it, never been used, which I am thankful for. Linens line the closet, which I put in the washer that's in the bathroom. Cleaning supplies are in the hall closet, along with washing detergent.

I'm wiping my hands on my shorts when I hear the knock. I open the door. His back faces me while he looks at the lake.

"Dad?" He turns to face me at the sound of his name.

"Your mother sent me with some food. She knew you didn't have anything here to eat." He's holding the bags out in front of him, as if to show me this is why he actually came.

Stepping inside, he sets the bag on the table and takes a seat, looking around.

I'm not sure what to say to him. I think he feels the same way. My chest hurts from the tightness built up inside, and I let out a forceful breath through barely parted lips.

"Rya, I'm sorry that I couldn't have taken those lashes for you. I've failed you as a father, as your protector." In this moment, my father looks so much older than he is. His head hangs down in his own guilt. All these years, I thought it was my shame that caused him so much hurt. It was his own shame of how he could not protect me better that caused the divide between us.

His hands go to his face, and he cries softly into them. His shoulders are shaking slightly—this is the first time I have ever seen him cry. My throat squeezes shut, burning tight with how utterly weak my father looks at this moment. My strong father that used to carry me around on his shoulders now looks like a broken old male. I feel as if it's my turn to carry him on my strong shoulders. Not only did this rejection affect me, it has affected my whole family. We have all been poisoned.

"Dad." My hand goes to his back, rubbing softly.

"I'm okay, Dad," I lie. It's the best lie I have ever told…*ever*.

CHAPTER 3

Valentine

The lake is like glass: tranquil, motionless, with steam rising up like fingered tendrils. Mother Nature gives me a picture of her stunning grace. Lazy clouds hang suspended in the sky, big and puffy, the early day hints at the warmth the sun will bring. Fish splashing above the water trying to catch the buzzing insects that hover just above the surface cause tiny ripples in the water. I need to get a hammock out front underneath the porch. I can picture it already: book in hand, one leg out swinging slowly while nature sings her song around me.

I will never get enough of this view. I try to make myself a promise to never let this be something I take for granted. I'm *lucky*; all I have to do is open the door and look outside…nature's healing sight.

A prickle of nerve endings, so powerfully pleasing, makes me still instantly. He is not an imposter; he is my moon's gift. I know exactly where to look.

Standing solitary on the opposite side of the lake, his wolf's eyes absorb me solely...*entranced*. It's hauntingly beautiful, his Wild surrounded by vapor, an apparition that appeals to my senses. With one blink of my eyes, he retreats back into the trees, into the shadows, until I'm alone again.

My heartbeat sounds like a drum, pounding against the inside of my chest. I can't do anything but stand and stare at the spot where he'd stood. Maybe I just imagined this, the steam causing a mirage.

If I don't move now, I'll be late for my first day at the clinic, and I don't think old Doc Peters would be thrilled with that. He's a stickler, very old school

It's about a fifteen-minute walk to the clinic. I don't mind walking; it calms my nerves for the big day, my skills on display for the doc to see. I have faith in everything I have learned. I'm clinically competent. With that thought, I stand a little taller. I'm confident in that, at least.

I knock on the door, and the healer greets me with a hug of welcome.

"Rya." A giant smile spreads on Aurora's face. The sixty-plus-year-old wolf's face dances in happiness. Her eyes are the color of sugar snap peas that reminds me of spring—fresh, new, *alive*.

"Look at you. Look how absolutely beautiful you turned out to be! I knew you would grow out of that gangly, all knees and elbows body." That is something I have never heard before. I'm not sure whether to be offended on how I used to look as a young juvenile or proud that I have finally grown into my mature form.

"Thank you." I'm unsure of how to respond to that.

"You smell very…healthy, Rya." Her hands squeeze my shoulders, and a sad smile turns down her face as her eyes reach mine, searching me.

"How are you?" She's not looking away after she says it. She really wants to know.

"I'm good." I give her the voice I have practiced for hours with.

The palm of her hand goes to my cheek, cupping it. Eyes that can see things others can't look softly into mine. All I can think is: don't cry, don't cry. Not on my first day, not within the first few minutes of my first real job. Don't cry, I can do this, I can *breathe*…just one breath in, one breath out…

The door to the clinic starts to open. Removing her hand, she stays close to me.

The male entering, eyes to the floor, has a shaved head. He looks up, and our eyes meet; always the same, an intake of breath as he takes in mine. Completely open mouthed, he stares before he slightly shakes his head and whispers an apology.

"Sorry, didn't mean to stare. They are *unusual*." He looks away with a slight pink to his cheeks.

"Dr. Valentine, this is the new midwife, Rya." Now it's my turn to be confused.

"Rya, nice to meet you." He sticks his hand out to welcome me the human way.

"Dr. Valentine, nice to meet you." Clasping his hand, I give it a quick shake before pulling away. I'm not in the habit of touching male wolves.

"Please, Rya, call me Dallas. We aren't very formal here." He looks at Aurora with a smile.

"Can I just ask, where is Dr. Peters?"

"Once I came and settled in, he decided it was time for him to retire. He's been gone maybe a year. Is that a problem?"

His voice is quiet, but I can hear him well. A day's growth on his face makes me think he might have had a late night, not wanting to shave this morning.

"No, I just wasn't told that we had a new doctor in the pack." It's a little uncomfortable between us; I'm not sure why.

His eyes avoid mine, looking anywhere but my face. Putting on his white lab coat, he looks the doctor part except he's young, only a few years older than me.

"Well, let's get you started. I'll show you to your office, to the birthing rooms." He shows me around this small clinic. Yet everything in here is top of the line, the best money can buy. Everything is available that one might need to keep the wolves alive.

Opening the door to the birthing rooms, I'm left speechless. Everything shiny and new, a big giant tub in the corner of each of the three rooms, bouncy balls, beds that turn into birthing chairs.

"This is amazing." I can't hide my excitement.

"The Alpha and Luna are very good with money, and they put a lot back into the pack." He seems to be impressed with those two wolves.

The office has a little weight scale for the pups and a stand-up scale for the mothers. A strong dark wooden desk, all new furniture. An examining table…

"The Luna had all the old crone's things moved out of here, replaced with all new stuff just for you."

"That was nice of her." His brow arches up, but he doesn't say anything else. My tone of voice could have been much nicer, hidden.

"Well, this is how it's going to work. I need to follow you with your assessments for a little while until the pack feels that I watched you enough. I really don't want to stare at pregnant females all day long. I have an aversion for those hormonal wolves, but a bigger aversion to their highly aggressive mates." I understand what he's saying: the males have to be restrained sometimes for a male doctor to help deliver the pup.

"Rya, there are two females due any day now; they will be coming in this morning. Usually, you'll work in the morning and have the afternoons off. The midwife did help me on occasion if I needed help and if the healer was busy. Are you okay with that?"

"Yes, where I was trained, that's exactly how it was done."

"Good. There are only about six pregnant females in the pack to date. They will all be in this week to see you. I'm sure you have lots of things you will need to organize the way you like it. If you need anything, any equipment that's not here, just tell me. I'll get it for you. If you have any difficulty or questions, please come to me."

"Thank you, Dr. Valent—"

Putting a hand up, he stops my next words. "Rya, just call me Dallas. Remember, we are not formal here."

"Okay, Dallas. Thank you."

Leaving me, he closes the door softly. Stacks of files sit on the desk, waiting for me to look through. Sitting behind the desk in *my office*, I take a big breath in, then out. I smile to myself because this feels right. I'm where I'm supposed to be.

The first heavily pregnant female arrives, the same female who told me there was no room at their table for me to sit on my first day back after my punishment. High school memories, the suffocating silence I endured as a juvenile, come crashing in. I have a choice: I can hold onto those years in bitterness or I can just let it go, start new, fresh...but always in my mind understand that I could never really be friends with those types of wolves.

Giving her a very soft, easy smile, I usher her into my examining room.

"Hello, Cora, how are you?" She looks nervous, rubbing her stomach.

"I'm good, Rya. How are you doing?" Her look is one of pity. Is this the look I'm going to have to get used to from the pack...eyes of *pity*?

"I'm good, Cora. Thank you for asking. Come inside. Doctor Valentine will be watching as I examine you. Is that okay with you?"

"Yes, it's fine." I put a hand up to her mate not to follow us in.

"I need to examine her properly, and so does the doctor." Her mate gives a low warning growl but sits in the seat outside the room in silent, behaved, fury.

"Please take off your shoes, and get undressed from the waist down. We'll be in soon." Closing the door, I try to act as professional as possible with her.

"I'd like to get your weight, check it from the previous one." I glance at her face and ankles, making sure she isn't retaining too much fluid.

Having her lay down on the examination table, I measure her abdomen. "Right on track. Excellent." Palpating her pup, I can feel the bum, head, and shoulders.

"She's already head down, won't be too long. I have to check you out down there. Is that okay?"

She giggles, and her face flushes nervously.

"I'm kind of embarrassed." She says it out loud as her legs spread underneath the cloth drape.

"Cora, don't be embarrassed. It's nothing I haven't seen before. You see one, you've seen them all." I give her a wink and a smile. Putting on a glove, I push her legs apart. I squeeze out some lubricant on my fingers, then feel inside her to see how ripe she is. Very good, already dilating and softening up.

Turning to Dallas, I say, "If you don't mind checking my assessment?" He does this as quickly as possible.

"Correct." He throws the glove in the garbage, washes his hands, then walks out the room.

As I help her into a sitting position, her hand goes on my shoulder.

"Rya, I just want to say—"

"It's okay, Cora. I'm okay, I have moved on with my life." It's my rehearsed line that I will use on everyone who asks me how I am. It's generic for everyone, but it will get what I want across…that I am okay.

"Good, I'm glad." Her smile is of someone who believes in lies.

Opening the door, I wave in her mate, who puts an arm around Cora. His lips brush the base of her marked neck before pulling way, smiling. A small curl of jealousy licks at my mind before I shove that thought away.

"So it should be very soon. Have you thought where you want to deliver, home or here?"

"Here. I think I would be more comfortable here," she says, her mate holding her hand in support.

"Perfect, I'll have everything ready for you. Just think, within the next few days, you will be holding your female." This time my smile reaches my eyes. There's nothing better than ushering new life into the world. I *love* what I do.

Her hands go to her belly again, rubbing it.

This is a new transition for the pack females, having a new midwife taking over. The first thing I need to build is *trust*…with all the females.

"I'm excited for you, Cora. This is going to be so wonderful. Trust me to help you through this." Helping her off the table, I give her a hug, putting my cheek against hers. I swallow down all those painful memories to give new, better memories a chance to be made.

The morning is spent filing and organizing how I

want things to be. The birth room is ready; I run through the supplies to be sure that I have everything. I look through all the files of the females I know. The midwife has information on all the female wolves of the pack. Her handwriting is legible in its own scratchy way.

The next pregnant female comes to see me, repeating the process. She leaves me with a smile on my face once she is gone. Two births in the next week should keep me busy for a few weeks with all the teaching that is needed with these new mothers-to-be.

It's surreal to think that I will be helping the females who turned their backs on me in my youth. I wonder if they feel any regret now, or do they even realize what an impact they have had on my life?

The call comes in the deep of night, when all things are still and sleeping, except for a pup that needs to give birth to a new mother.

I make it there before them, turning on the lights. Dallas strolls in with tired eyes. He has dark blue scrub bottoms on with a matching top; my outfit is the same. My hair is tied away from my face.

"Coffee?" he questions.

"No, I'm fine. Thank you."

"I'll let you lead this. If you need my help, just ask. Otherwise, you're on your own. I'm just an observer, okay, Rya?"

"All right."

Cora enters, walking slowly, stopping for a minute while a contraction rolls through her. She grits her teeth, holding her breath in.

"Cora, breathe out. Let your breath out. Don't hold it in." Her mate supports her body with his. He looks more frightened than her.

"Let's get you into a gown and check you out." The contraction ends.

She doesn't get far when the next heavy contraction makes her abdomen hard and taut. She's shaking with the force. A muffled cry goes up to the moon in agony. He tries to make her walk forward.

"Stop touching me!" she hisses at him. Her mate looks hurt with the cutting words.

Getting her undressed and into the birthing bed is a monumental task. She is not laboring well; her groans and grunts are turning into screams and pleas for help. She's begging the moon to help her. I smile to myself. All females have different thresholds of pain; obviously, this one has no threshold.

My job is to support her, to help guide her through this.

The hours roll by. Dallas is on his laptop doing work. He's really not paying any attention to the birth, letting me head this ship. The male in the room eyes him every so often, growls, and steps his way.

"If you can't behave, you need to leave." My voice is very stern with her mate. He needs to control himself. I look at Dallas; he seems like he could take care of himself in a fight. He looks like he trains every day, even though he's a doctor.

Dallas pays no mind to the male that's posturing his unhappiness that another male is in the room with his mate at such a vulnerable time.

Cora's head swings from side to side, tears streaming down her face, her breathing coming out ragged.

"Not another one!" she cries out, holding my hand.

"Breathe with me, Cora. Breathe in and a long breath out. We're almost there, not much longer. This won't last. Breathe in and a long breath out. Good job, you're doing so well." Her eyes meet mine, sweat saturating the sheets.

"I'm going to check you again, okay?" She's starting to crown. It's time to push.

"The next contraction, we need to start pushing her out, okay?" The bed is shifted into a sitting position, rails going up to help her bear down and push the pup out.

Eyes closed, she tenses up with the oncoming contraction.

"Breathe, Cora. Big breath in, that's it. Now push down. That's it, push her out." Her face is red, the vein in her face popping out with the exertion.

Her mate has her hand, rubbing her shoulder, encouraging her to push. Kissing her cheek.

For the next thirty minutes, this female pushes with all her strength.

With the sunrise, a pup slips out of its mother's nest. The tiny first cry of the newborn brings smiles to all our faces. The mother no longer hurts my ears with her screams. Her mate beams proudly as a new father does.

He gets to cut the cord, then hands the infant off to Dallas to look over. She delivers the placenta, and I inspect her to make sure she didn't suffer any damage from the birth. She looks good; she should heal up quickly.

Covering her with a light blanket, I walk toward Dallas, who is writing down weight and length in this female's chart.

"Good job, Rya." He steps aside for me to clean the pup. Swaddling the young in a blanket, I then bring her to her mother, whose open arms are waiting.

These next twenty-four hours are busy: the health teaching on how to breastfeed properly, how to change a diaper, how to clean the tiny pup. Making sure Mom is doing well, no more bleeding. Once I think they've gotten the hang of it, I let the male take his mate and newborn home. I'll see them every day for the next week, just to make sure both mother and pup are doing well.

Friday has me knocking on Cora's door for my routine visit. Kennedy is the one who opens the door, holding the young pup in her arms. Not looking directly at her, I keep my head down slightly. It's easier for me this way. I don't want to look at someone I'm jealous of.

Sitting on the couch next to Cora is the Luna. *I can do this.* I need to just start getting used to this. They will always visit new mothers. This is just how it is.

"Good afternoon, Luna Catherine, Kennedy." I nod in both of their directions, and my voice doesn't crack. It stays solid and comfortable, even to my ears.

"Cora, I brought you some chicken soup and bread." This helps a female in the first week, not having to make food. It's good on their stomachs to not have anything too heavy to digest.

"Thank you, Rya. Your soups are so good." Cora gets up off the couch, pressing her cheek to mine in greeting.

"How are you feeling?"

"Good. I feel so much better."

"How's the breastfeeding going? Any issues?"

"No, I think I'm getting the hang of it." I assess this female in front of me for any hidden lies. She just has very tired eyes that stare back, but nothing else.

"Well, I'll just weigh her and let you get on with your day."

I put my bag on the table and take out the weight. Kennedy hands me the female. I have to try not to shake, because all I can smell is him. He's all over her. A quick glance at her neck and it's all red and irritated. It looks as if it hurts. Males, they love to *bite*.

I have to get used to this, just another hurdle to get over.

"Rya, how are you? Do you have everything you need at the clinic?" The Luna's now standing beside me with gentle eyes. I look away, concentrating on stripping the female pup from her clothes and diaper.

"Yes, thank you." Weighing the infant, I write the information down in my notebook. I wrap her back up nice and warm. I give her a little smell. I love the scent of newborns.

"Cora, she's doing perfectly fine. Dr. Valentine wants you to bring her in next week. I'll be done with the both of you unless you need me for anything. Just call."

"Rya, thank you so much for everything. I don't know what I would have done without you. Thank you." She's the one who wraps her arms around me with tears in her eyes in gratitude.

"You did all the work. I just helped guide Mother Nature along. I mean it. Call if you need anything."

"Goodbye, Luna, Kennedy." Bowing slightly in a show of respect, I ease out of the house that holds his scent.

My legs are shaking so bad that I almost have a hard time walking away. Why does this have to be so hard? I'm trying to compose myself when the door opens again. It's the Luna.

She closes the door behind her, making her way to me. I'm trying with everything I have to control my emotions.

Turning my back on her, I close my eyes, focusing on breathing. I just can't control myself at the moment.

"Rya."

"Yes, Luna." I stop walking with my back to her, hands squeezing the material of my bag, waiting for what she has to say.

"I just needed to say good job. Dr. Valentine said that you're a natural, that you have been moon-blessed with your gift." Dallas is just trying to smooth all the females' fur down, placing his trust in me.

"Thank you, Luna." I can't turn around to meet her eyes. My voice is so shaky, it cracks with emotion.

"Rya, if you ever need to talk—"

"No, I'm fine, Luna Catherine. Sometimes I just have a moment, but I'm fine. Thank you for your concern."

"Cathy, are you ready to go?" Kennedy asks. I say no more, walking in the opposite direction from where they are going.

"Rya, barbecue on Sunday. I expect you there," she commands. I don't acknowledge the invitation. Instead, I just keep walking without turning back.

Making my way back to the cottage is a half hour walk, but the breeze feels good in the heat of the day. I left my windows and door open to try and rid the house of the old wolf's scent that still lingers in some corners.

She died over a month ago. It feels weird to occupy something that belonged to another for so long.

She planted a garden in the spring that's been overrun with weeds. My goal is to return it to the way she intended it to be, a harvest of nature.

The soil is rich and black; it clings underneath my nails. Pulling weeds is no joke. It's tedious, and my back hurts from being bent over for so long.

Slowly, this garden is taking shape. Already there is an abundant yield. I can give away so much, canning the rest. I'm excited about this prospect.

All the work this represents will keep my mind busy so it doesn't float to things that can't be changed.

CHAPTER 4

Sunday

A nervous feeling bubbles in my stomach at the thought of actually seeing him again. Sitting once again in my car, I give myself a stern talking to. My parents will be there; my sisters will be there. I will not embarrass the people I love *again*. It was so much easier out of sight, out of mind.

Opening the car door, I end up closing it again. Every time I open it, all I can smell is him. It's a drowning feeling, and I am unable to catch my breath. My eyes fill with water. It's such a struggle not to break down.

Why me? Why can't I just feel numb to him? Why does he affect me so much? How do I not affect him? How can he fight this so easily? I pound on the steering wheel. I feel as if someone is pushing on my chest. The pressure gets heavier and heavier until I really start to feel lightheaded.

With my head down, I just sit there, unable to really find the motivation to move. Knuckles tapping on the window draw my eyes up. Dallas is looking at me, our eyes meet, and he doesn't look away. Opening the door for me to get out, he still holds my gaze.

"I just need a minute, Dallas." I try to close the door again, and he stops me from doing that.

"I've been watching you for the last hour in your car, talking to yourself. I think you were even answering back." He opens the door wider for me to get out.

"I'm sorry, this is so silly." I still can't get out of the car.

"I don't think it is. I think it's really sad for you. I think that you are the strongest person I know." His hand reaches for mine, the one that is still clenching the steering wheel.

"I don't feel strong," I whisper, barely audible, even to my ears.

"You are." He lets me sit a moment more before he pulls me out.

"All right, I'm ready. I have some stuff for the pack in the trunk. Can you help me carry it in?" I step away from him.

"Sure." Opening the trunk of the car, I have boxes of veggies from the garden. All fresh without the smell of pesticides, sun-ripened…so *healthy*.

Carrying the boxes of produce in front of me, I try to have the cardboard act as a shield from his stare. It doesn't work; I feel it instantly as soon as Dallas and I round the corner of the house into the backyard. I don't even have to look to see where he's at. My body just knows. My soul is trying to touch his. It's as if it's leaning out a window with its arms out, fingertips stretched completely straight, trying to get closer to him.

I turn my body away from his, and my bare arm brushes against the doctor's skin. We both look down at the spot where our flesh touched, aware of the contact we just made.

"Sorry about that," I say, taking a step away from him.

"No, that's okay. Let's put these down and maybe get us both a drink?" His voice is gentle, yet at the same time he gives me direction on what to do next.

"Good idea." My back burns with his eyes against my skin.

I put them on a table with a sign that says *please take*. The wolves should love this, especially the ones who don't have a garden. Nothing like fresh veggies.

The wind lifts the hem of my skirt slightly, exposing my bare thighs. I can see Dallas out of the corner of my eyes, looking at me. He doesn't linger for too long.

"I brought some beer. Would you like one?" He's going to a cooler, opening it up.

"Are you sure? If you have enough, I would like one."

"I have more than enough for *you*." He hands the open bottle to me, and I take the first drink. The liquid is cold against my throat.

"Thanks." With my back to my mate, I take in the gathering. The whole pack is out enjoying themselves, laughing and carrying on, the adults playing bean bag toss, lawn darts. There is a game of volleyball to the side in a pit of sand that replaced grass; it looks very official.

"Are you hungry? Do you want something to eat?" Now, this is extremely embarrassing.

"I can't eat until everyone else does. I can't even sit with the pack." I look at a solitary table slightly away from the main group…*my place*.

"What are you talking about?" That's the loudest I have ever heard his voice go.

"When I was punished, I had to eat last, and I couldn't eat with the pack anymore. I'm still last."

"Come with me, now." He walks us toward the Alpha and Luna while I start to backpedal. He's muttering something under his breath that I can't make out.

"Rya, how are you?" Luna Catherine and the Alpha call out. My head instantly goes down, my breath coming out a little harsher.

"Good, thank you for asking." I just give them the generic line everyone gets.

"How's she doing at the clinic?" the Alpha asks Dr. Valentine.

"She's fitting in really well with the team. She's an extremely wonderful asset to the pack, and we are all very lucky to have someone like her." The gentle pressure of fingertips touch my lower back; this is the first time I have ever been touched there by a male. I cringe slightly. He withdraws his hand, letting it rest at his side. Warm molten lava slowly slides down from the tip of my head, caressing my shoulders; heat burns so pleasurably into my hips that I have to stifle a moan. My ass heats up, the exposed skin of my thighs tingling with his stare. I have to catch myself; my head wants to roll back, and my legs become liquid jelly.

"Good, glad to hear that." I don't even look at the Alpha when he's talking, preferring to just keep silent. It's just better not to talk. I wonder if my cheeks are flushed.

"Rya, you look very pretty." I still don't meet their eyes.

"Thank you, Luna Catherine." I don't say anything else.

"I just have one question. Why is Rya eating last? Why is she not allowed to sit with her own family?" The doc is seething mad, shaking inside his skin.

"I have no idea what you're talking about, Dr. Valentine."

"Rya was just telling me that she has to eat last!" Wolves turn their gazes our way with the doc's raised voice.

"Rya, what's he talking about?" I can hear the confusion in the Alpha's voice.

"You never removed your punishment from me," I say quietly.

"What are you talking about?" Luna Catherine's voice questions her mate, not in a nice way.

"He never removed my punishment."

"Rya, that was years ago. I only meant that to be a week."

Now it's my turn to gasp.

"A week. You meant it to last just a week? You never told me that. All those years of eating last, not being able to eat with my family at pack functions. You just forgot to tell me that my punishment was done?"

"Unbelievable," Dallas hisses out.

"Rya, I am so sorry. I thought I told you." He takes my hand in his, getting on his knees in front of the entire eyes of the pack. "I thought I told you. I thought…Please forgive me. It was a mistake." I can see the top of his head as he bows to me.

"I can't believe you did that to this poor female. How could you have forgotten to take her off of punishment?" The Luna's face is inflamed with her fury. I can see canines descending in her rage.

"Please, Rya, forgive me. It doesn't make up for it." He's still at my feet on bended knee.

Touching his head, I say, "I forgive you." Quickly, I pull my hand away. I can't make a scene again.

He gets up quickly, trying to look at my face, but I keep my head bowed.

"Please—" I stop the Luna from talking any further. I can't stomach anything else. All those years of isolation because he forgot that I was on punishment. I had to eat by myself for two years, pretending to look busy in the library with studying so no one really saw how alone I was. I was just a ghost no one cared about, all because he *forgot*…I was just a little juvenile whose mate rejected her. Whose pack turned on her. Whose Alpha forgot about her.

It's in this moment I feel him coming nearer, approaching slowly, cautiously. I smell *him*. My knees shake, threatening once again to fold on themselves.

All this emotion brings me back in time.

His scent surrounds me almost like the first time coming into the school, smelling him, asking if I could talk with him for just a minute, alone, without her there. To just let me *talk* to him. When he wouldn't let go of her hand, I started crying then. He knew what I was to him, yet he didn't let go of her hand.

My chest is once again in a vise, squeezing the breath out. She just stood there watching me, not saying a thing. *"Please,"* I cried, *"please look at me."* I tried to grab his hand. I tried to make him look at my eyes. I fell down on my knees, begging him, grabbing onto his pant leg. A crowd formed around us. Some were even laughing at me. He pulled his leg back, but I held onto the material.

All it took was one word from her: "Stop." My wolf bared its teeth, and time ceased...Hit after hit rained down on her face, breaking her jaw. I tried to crush her skull with my bare hands, but I wasn't strong enough then. I am now.

I'm not a life taker. I am a life bringer.

"Rya." It's the first time I have heard my name from his mouth. I actually stagger, dropping to a knee...the tears, they just come. My whole body is weeping, and I lose all the control that I have worked years on. Everything vanishes with just my name coming from his lips. I'm full-out sobbing, and I can't even pick myself off the ground. *Why?*

No one says a word...silence, complete silence.

This is not the picture I saw in my mind for myself. This is not how I wanted my first time seeing him to go.

Both of my hands are on the ground, clutching

the earth to my flesh. I can see his shoes, his calves; they look so strong. Goosebumps ascend on his flesh where my gaze falls, his thighs thick, his defined quads just peeking out of his shorts. I see their hands clasped together. This is just like a replay of my past.

I try to get up, but I fall back down. A gasp comes out of my mouth. I watch as his hand lets hers go to try and help me up off the ground. He takes a step toward me, her hand holding onto his forearm to try and stop him. He takes another step in my direction, and she pulls him back toward her.

On my own, I get myself off the ground, standing, not looking at anyone. I hold my shoulders back, raising my head, and my gaze travels up his chest. He's shaking now. My eyes reach his neck, mouth, nose. His eyes, pine green, stare hard at me. A moment passes between us…nothing else but he and I…

"*Rya.*" Again my name comes from his lips, again my legs shake…A hurricane is lashing the inside of my body…

I say nothing. Instead, I turn my back on him and walk away. I walk until I reach my car. Getting in, I struggle to find the right key for the ignition. Finally finding it, I drive away, not even looking in the rearview mirror for fear I will see his eyes again.

Instead, I look ahead to what's in front of me.

CHAPTER 5

Somebody

Grey clouds hide the sun's light, and an eerie stillness settles around the lake. Even the birds are silent. Growling thunder gives its warning that a raucous storm is about to be released.

Instead of walking, I decide to take the car, not trusting that I can make it to the clinic before the rain comes.

The wind starts to rustle the leaves of the trees as I reach the clinic. The first few fat drops of rain hit my face before I walk through the front door. I feel my cheeks redden with the embarrassment of yesterday's loss of control.

Aurora is there sipping a morning tea, the hot vapor of the steam hitting her face as she peers down into the cup. She looks up at me with eyes that see into me, not at me. Into me.

"You're a mess." Looking down at myself, I thought I looked presentable today, nice and tidy. Professional in every aspect. Touching my hair, I wonder if it has come out of its braid.

"Rya, what happened yesterday—"

"Aurora, it's okay. It won't happen again. I just lost control for a second. It was the first time I've seen him since I've been back. I'll be more prepared next time. I'll have better control." I try to say this so calmly as if this is true.

"I think we need to schedule some time to talk, just you and me. I know you're a lot sicker than you think. You can't see it, but I can. Your mind is not well. Your body is so healthy, but your mind needs help. I will help you. Just like you can help those pregnant females with their births, I can help you. Let me help you, Rya."

I wasn't expecting this first thing in the morning; my legs are glued to my spot. Eyes of light green stare at me, waiting for something to come out of my mouth. A flash of light from the window, followed by a loud boom that feels as if it's inside the room, makes me jump slightly. The lights flicker on and off before staying on.

"The first step, Rya, is admitting you need help. Nothing is shameful in needing help. What's shameful is you living your life the way you are. Your potential is limitless. The moon has blessed you. It's my job now to help you see this." The first stray tear leaks out.

"Where were you when I was a juvenile? Where were you?" I accuse her. She could have helped me then.

"Sometimes good people are meant to suffer. You learn from it, grow from it, become better from it. Now the suffering needs to stop before it eats you and you can't come back from it." Another flash of lightning lights the inside of the clinic.

"The first thing is to admit you're not fine. That's the first thing you need to do. Tell me, Rya, *how are you*?" She holds my eyes with hers, waiting. The storm is raging outside, shaking the earth with its violence. Trees' limbs bend back and forth, and hard rain beats against the windows.

She's right. If I really look at myself, she's right. I just don't know how to help myself anymore. I want to feel something other than this. I want to be able to just move on with my life…to be free of this suffocation, the constriction around my life that has been devouring me like a snake, slowly, little by little.

"I'm not fine." That's all I say, nothing more. I can't say anything else. Getting up from her spot, she pulls me into a hug. Her cheek presses against mine. She holds me to her for just a minute as the brutal power of nature unleashes the Wild.

We stand together until the fury of the storm subsides. It leaves faster than it came.

"Good, that's all for today," she whispers in my ear and pats me on my back. She releases me, stepping away. I don't feel any different, but I know that this may be my beginning.

Looking over my charts for the day in my office, I see only two females will be here. Then I will make my rounds to the two new mothers, just to make sure they really are doing well.

A tap on the door reveals Dallas looking down at me. He stares at my eyes again before he catches himself, pulling his gaze away and looking at the picture I put on the wall of the first young one that I delivered in my pack. I feel proud of this fact. Soon, I hope to have my office lined with little newborn faces.

"How are you doing? I stopped by your place yesterday. I knocked, but I guess maybe you were out for a run?" He doesn't come completely into my office, just lingers outside the door with a soft expression on his face. Maybe he's waiting for me to invite him *in*.

"I'm sorry, I was home. I just didn't want to talk to anyone. I'm really embarrassed at how I behaved. It was difficult for me. Thank you for stopping by. That was nice of you." After getting home from the barbecue, locking the doors, making sure no lights were on, I just sat at the edge of the bed, balling the covers in my hands. Staring at the white wall, I cursed myself to the moon. If I was only *better,* if I was *more*. I wallowed in my own pity party. The knocking started all different types of knocking. I could smell my parents; I could smell my sisters. I knew that the Alpha and Luna were at my door. Even Cora came. I just stayed in my room with the daylight fading from the sky, until nothing but darkness could be seen through my window.

I just sat there on edge, holding myself in place, not moving. If I were to move, I would break. Deeper into the night, a single knock on my door came. My body started to shake with who it was standing there, waiting for me to open the door. To invite him into my home. He stayed there, waiting. I sat on my bed, waiting for him to leave, and eventually he did.

"It was very difficult for all the mated wolves to watch. You have nothing to be embarrassed about." He's trying to catch my eyes, but I refuse to look at him. "Rya, anytime you want to talk—"

"Thanks, Dallas, I appreciate that."

"All right, if you need anything, you know where my office is." Putting my head down, I pretend to look at a chart.

"Thanks." He's gone after my words come out of my mouth.

I just need some air. There's something about a settled storm, just after the wind whips the loose leaves off the trees. The way the earth smells fresh, renewed. The grass looks greener, the birds sing louder, and the sun seems brighter with its warm light.

A car pulling into the parking lot attracts my attention, black-tinted windows not allowing me to see who's inside. The door opens, and the Luna steps out, along with her young juvenile daughter, who looks down at the ground, tight-lipped.

"Rya, I wanted to stop by and see you—"

"Luna Catherine." I bow my head slightly to her. "I'm working. Now is not a good time."

"You're right, you are working, but I didn't come for our talk. Kimberly has an appointment with you this morning." She puts her hand on her daughter's shoulder as Kimberly picks at the cuticle of her fingernail, looking down in shame.

"Please, come in." I hold the door open so they can step into the clinic.

Walking them toward my office, I gesture them inside. "Please, sit down." I take a seat, opening her empty chart.

"So, Kimberly, how far along do you think you are?" She keeps her head down, not looking up.

"I'm two months." I don't see any claim marks on her neck, nothing that says she has a mate beside a pup in her belly.

"Do you mind if I ask you a few questions before I examine you?" I'm trying to be as professional with her as possible.

She looks toward her mother, then back at me.

"Luna Catherine, do you mind waiting outside while I talk with Kimberly? I have to ask her some personal questions. It won't take long, but I do need you to step out, please." This time, I meet the Luna's eyes directly. She might be over me in the pack, but in this office, I have authority. I will not back down. My pregnant females will always come first.

She doesn't look away. Neither do I. Finally, she gets up off the chair. Her daughter is open mouthed at our interaction, looking from my face to her mother's. The Luna cannot hide the smile that's spread wide, making her look so beautiful. "I'll just wait outside."

"Kimberly, how old are you?"

"Sixteen."

"Was this your first heat?"

"Yes." She's picking at her fingernails.

"Did you want to get pregnant?"

"No." She starts shaking her head vigorously. "I just didn't think it would happen." Her poor little lips start to tremble. It must be very scary for her, being so young to have the responsibility of a new life inside her.

"Did you not take the proper precautions?" She shakes her head no, focusing out the window. I try to mask my surprise at this. All the young females should know better when they are in their fertile times. This gives me a good idea to gather all the young adolescent females for a health lesson on proper precautions and how to use them.

"It was my first time, Rya. I was where all the females go to ride out the heat, but the door was unlocked. He got in." She's still looking at her nails as if they're the most important thing that can hold her attention. Whoever was responsible for the door should be shot with silver.

"All right, Kimberly, let's get your weight and some measurements. Then we will do an ultrasound, have a proper look at him." I can smell the male inside her; he's strong already. "Where's your mate at?"

"He just left for University. He won't be back until his first semester is done." This is going to be tough on her without her mate by her side.

"Okay, let's get your mother. We'll do an ultrasound, then you can be on your way." Leaving her on the table, I go get the Luna. She's sitting with Aurora, having tea and laughing like two old friends.

"You can come in now." Turning on my heels, I don't wait for her to follow.

Back in the examination room, I ask her to lift her shirt up, then put the cold jelly on her lower abdomen. I start to look around to find the little guy. The Luna enters the darkened room, standing by her daughter's side. It doesn't take long to locate the forming young.

"There we are. He doesn't look like much now, but just wait." I turn on the sound so they can hear the rapid heartbeat clearer. The Luna has tears in her eyes; so does Kimberly. What a nice moment for mother and daughter. I *wish* I could give my mother this moment. Watching the Luna bend down and kiss her daughter's head makes me smile. She will have the support she needs during this time.

Printing several pictures for the both of them, I wipe away the sticky jelly from her lower abdomen and help her sit up. I think to myself this could have been my nephew.

"All done." Both of them are smiling at the grainy pictures.

I walk out to the front desk with them. Aurora also acts as a secretary, booking an appointment with the doctor, her, and myself.

"All right, let's see, I think we should see you in two months, all right?"

"What day? I have to go away for a week to visit another pack. It has to be either before or after that week." The Luna is looking at the dates on the calendar.

"Still hunting?" Aurora's voice questions out.

"Always." Luna Catherine and Aurora have a silent moment between themselves before Kennedy barges into the office.

"Oh, I thought I was late." She sounds breathless, like she was in a rush to get here. Her curly hair is a vision of beauty. The way her dress clings to her body shows off her slim hips and long

47

legs. No wonder my male loves her. She's a vision of absolute perfection, her makeup done as if she had professional artists do it.

"We're just finishing up," the Luna says.

"I thought you said the appointment was at ten, Cathy?"

"Did I? No, you must have heard me wrong. I said nine-thirty, Kennedy." Looking at Kennedy, I notice that her neck is not as red and irritated as before. As if it's been left alone…

"Well, when's the next appointment? I don't want to miss it." She really looks upset.

"It's in two months. We'll be away when she goes. Her father will take her."

"I don't need to go with you, Cathy. I can just stay here this time, to keep an eye on Kimmy and my little pup."

"No, Kennedy, I need you with me when we visit the other packs." The Luna's voice is tight but restrained.

The Luna and Aurora share another look together.

Kennedy doesn't even acknowledge my presence. She won't even look at me as she walks away outside.

"Kimberly, if you have any questions or need anything, or if you just feel weird, please come and see me before our appointment. Or if you just need to talk about things."

"You're so very kind, Rya. We are so thankful you're back. Would it be okay if I stop by this afternoon at your house? I think maybe we need to have a talk. Just you and I." Luna Catherine's voice holds a command in it. She won't take no for an answer.

"I'm busy this afternoon, sorry." I don't want to sit and talk with her. I have nothing to say to them.

"Rya—" Dallas comes out of his office, standing just outside his door.

"Yes, Dr. Valentine?" He's holding a bundle of paper in his hands.

"Here's all the papers that need to be filled out. Thanks again for helping me this afternoon." He hands me the stack of charts, our fingertips touching while he hands me them. A flush creeps along his neck with the contact. I have to look away from him, but I can smell him…

"Well, Rya, another day maybe, when you aren't too busy." She doesn't say it to me; she's staring down Dallas, a hard look in her eyes, the wolf ascending. I can feel vibrations off her skin that she's sending his way. He holds her stare for a moment before turning around, shutting his office door.

Both of them leave as I shut the door behind them, thankful that they left.

Dallas comes out of his office and leans against the doorframe, arms crossed over his chest. A keen smile spreads wide across his face.

"You better watch yourself with her, Dr. Valentine." Aurora gives Dallas a bright smile.

"What can she do to me? I'm the doctor!" They both laugh at that. The way he laughs is contagious, almost pulling me into a laugh…almost.

Dallas takes the stack of papers from my hand, bringing them back into his office.

"If you really need help…"

"No, this is all garbage that needs to be shredded. Thanks, anyway. You have a good afternoon, Rya. See you tomorrow."

"You too, Dallas. Thank you for that." My eyes meet his in thanks, and another blush creeps on his face. I find that cute in a flattering way.

Aurora comes into my office, sipping a fresh cup of tea.

"Don't you think it's sweet of Luna Catherine, always bringing Kennedy with her to meet other packs, molding her for her future role as a Luna? You know what I find really nice? That all the Lunas of the other packs hold a nice welcome dinner for them. All the unmated male pack members are expected to show up so they can meet this future Luna. Catherine has been dragging her around for years doing this. She refers to it as *hunting*." Aurora blows on her cup of tea before taking a sip, eyes watching mine. "You didn't hear that from me." Before I get to say a word, she turns around, leaving me open mouthed.

After finishing with my work, I decide to walk home, just in case the Luna drives by and doesn't see my car. I don't want her stopping by.

Nothing but little puddles are left in the wake of the storm. Everything else is dry underneath the sun's hot eye.

Walking down my driveway, keys jingling in my hands, I notice how the wind lifts the willow tree's hanging limbs in a gentle dance, swaying back and forth. Green eyes glint at me in the shadow of the tree.

Stepping into the sun, he looks like a vision…a horrible, wonderful vision…

"Rya."

CHAPTER 6

Sliding In, Falling Out

Static crackles between the two of us…
He doesn't move.
He doesn't speak.
He doesn't do anything but stare at me.

His eyes capture mine, and everything slides away. Nothing else exists, just him.

A chemical reaction of the purest, simplest elements merge together, creating something that feels combustible. This moment will always loiter in my mind. This one real moment between the two of us without witnesses.

He begins to step toward me, one long stride at a time. Watching, he inhales deeply, eyes closing, a shudder quivering his muscles. Another step toward me, his hands shake like my heart. Core muscles tighten. My tendons are taut, my bones quaking with the assault inside my body. His muscles are contracting, causing spasms under his exposed skin. Another step toward me. I can actually hear his erratic heartbeat inside his chest. Our bodies sync with each other.

Bliss so pure runs up my spine, wrapping around my shoulders, hugging me in its embrace.

I let my eyes caress every curve, every edge of his body. I try to ingrain every detail of skin, the curve of his lips, broad shoulders, muscular neck...my scent giving off just how much I appreciate what's standing in front of me. His eyes are blazing bright green, the desire pouring off him in waves. He sucks a breath in...

This is how it should have been for us...this moment. This is what was meant to happen.

Finally, he's standing right in front of me. His head angles down, and my head angles up, eyes not leaving each other. His violent shivers shake the both of us. Just an inch separates our bodies. Dipping his head down toward my neck, he inhales. Growls vibrate his expanding chest as they percuss into mine.

My heart flutters wildly, and his nose almost touches my flesh. Lips are so close to my skin, and his fingertip almost touches me, just hovering...waiting...Can he feel my breath on them? He pulls himself away, just a step back, but it feels like we're now standing miles apart. If I were quick enough, I could claim him now. No one would look down on that...*except him*.

Opening up his mouth, letting a long breath out, he looks me in the eyes. By the way he is squaring his shoulders, I know this is going to hurt.

"I love her, but I can't stop myself from wanting you. I can't stop myself from wanting to touch you.

I want to stop myself, but I can't." His agony hurts my ears with the pain he's feeling, the conflict his body and mind are waging within himself.

"She's what I love, but you're what I *need*." He takes another long inhale into his lungs, and his eyes close for just a fraction of a moment before they open into the color of a deep dark forest canopy. My turn to reach for him, fingertips extending, but he's standing just a feather's breath too far.

"I don't want to hurt her," he whispers.

"What about me?" I ask him back.

He can't answer me.

My heart breaks.

The magic between us fades.

"I understand *Clayton*." His fists clench, his canines descend, and his jaw start to take on an irregular shape as his muscles start shifting into his wolf's form. He gives a grunt, shaking his head back and forth, pain etched across his face. He's trying to prevent a shift from happening, fighting with his wolf nature...

"Stop."

He says this out loud, not to me, but to himself before his face goes back to his skin side.

"She's always been there. She's all I have ever known. Ever had." He's trying to explain himself.

"I have known no one," I counter back. He nods his head at me as if he can even grasp the understanding of this. He *has someone.*

"I grew up with her. She was my first kiss, my first love, my first everything." His eyes aren't leaving me; his truth is *killing me.*

"I never had a first kiss. I never had a first love. I never had any of that. I was saving all of that for *you.*" His eyes close, looking so pained.

"I'm so sorry," he quavers. My hand goes over my mouth, a sob trying to escape from my hand that's trying to keep my cries silent, trying with every ounce of dignity to control myself...I just can't.

"What's so wrong with me? I could have been everything to you..." The words are hardly recognizable with the crack of my voice, the sobs pouring out. My chest burns with the emotions I'm feeling.

"Rya, nothing is wrong with you. You're perfect in every single way. *It's me.*" He touches his heart. "I just can't let her go, but I can't stop myself from being here with you." He clutches the material of his shirt in his hand. I want to be that material.

"Since you came back, I can't get you out of here." He taps his head.

"I want to touch you, but I want to hold her." He raises his hand up so his fingertip almost brushes my lips. I can feel the electricity from his *almost* touch tingling my lips.

"I want to kiss her, but I can't, because all I can think about is kissing you. It's so messed up." His soul is starting to open up to me. I can feel it reaching for me, trying to pull me in.

"It was easier for me when we were younger. You looked like a little girl with nothing that I wanted except your soul. Even then, I wanted your soul in mine," he says, letting his voice whisper the last words out.

"I thought that I could fight it, that it wasn't that hard. You went away, which made it much easier for me. After the first year, I could pretend you were never here. But then you came back. I always knew you would. I just didn't expect this. I never expected this…You are the most beautiful thing ever." His hands are clenched so tight that small droplets of blood start to splatter on the green grass.

"You stand in front of me looking at me with those eyes; I can't stop thinking about them. I want to lay you down and just stare at them. I want so much from you, yet at the exact same time, I have so much from Kennedy. She has given me so much. She is my best friend, my lover, my everything. I can't just give that up. I want to for you, but I can't for her.

"I'm sorry. This is how I feel." He just studies me, waiting for my words to tumble out.

Inhaling for a long moment, he lets his breath out slow through parted lips, tongue licking them, moistening them. I want to groan with the sight I have at the moment.

"I can smell you, Rya. I can catch you on the breeze when I least expect it. You smell innocent, as if your skin is waiting for mine." He takes just the tiniest step toward me. I could reach out now and touch him if I want to. I don't. Instead, I take his scent into me, inhaling long and slow. I smell the complete maleness of him, the sweet desire of him.

"I can smell you, Clayton, yet underneath all your layers, I can smell Kennedy. I can smell her in every pore, every crack of your skin, *everywhere*.

I'm not sure she could ever really fade away from your smell." I want to weep with this thought.

"I don't want her scent to fade off my skin, but I want to be on your skin."

"Does she know you're here?" I wait for his answer.

"No." Shame fills his face.

"You need to leave me alone, Clayton. I can't do this. I'm not the other female. I'm not that type of person." My eyes are stinging from all my crying.

"I can't." He's looking at me again. "I'm sorry. I want to leave you alone, but I just can't. I can't stop loving her, either. I can't turn that off."

"You can't have the both of us."

"I know that."

"Then I will make that choice for you. Stop looking at me, stop following me around, and stop trying to contact me. I need you to just leave. Turn around and walk away like you did that day. Go to her. Go to where you belong." He doesn't move.

It's my move, and I choose to give him my back, taking the first real step away. It's not forced out of embarrassment or to not cause a scene. This is my choice to walk away willingly. In a way, I can breathe just a touch easier than before.

I turn around one last time. He's still standing in that same spot, unable to move away from me.

"Screw you, Clayton, for doing this to me." I'm not malicious in my words; they aren't harsh. I don't scream them out. They are just my soft truth.

Closing my door, I breathe out a slow, painful breath.

The mirror above the basin of the sink holds my

reflection in the glass. The image staring back has red, puffy eyes and tired lungs. I watch as the smallest breeze finds its way in to gently blow the delicate curtains up. Staring at myself, I just see a female who is only trying to exist. Nothing more, nothing less, just *existing*.

Stepping into the shower, I wash away the faint layer of his scent that was trying to cling to me. Down the drain, the soapy water takes him away, nothing to linger, nothing to remind me that he's been here.

My walk back to the clinic is quiet. Nature's background noise is soothing to my soul. Dallas is there locking the door, head down, a backpack slung over his one shoulder as if he's just getting done with school. He walks away in the opposite direction, his hand in his pocket. I watch as he goes by my car; a fingertip traces the front, gliding across the length of it before ending at the back. He puts his hand back in his pocket. Even strides carry him away. I just stand there looking at him before I decide to call out to him.

"Hey, Dallas! Do you need a ride home?" I jingle my keys in my hand, waiting for an answer.

Surprised, his smiling eyes meet mine.

"If you're going that way, sure."

"I'm not sure where you even live, but I can drive you. I'm not really busy at the moment."

"Thanks, I appreciate this." He's at the side of my car. Opening it, I let him in. He's nervous but maintaining appearances.

Rolling down his window, he takes some deep breaths in as the wind swirls around inside between us.

"Turn right here, just at the end of this road." I pull off the main road onto a dirt road winding like a snake into the forest. A small cottage just like mine sits solitary on the edge of the lake. It's on the opposite side from my house.

I wasn't expecting this. I thought he would have something grand, doctor-ish. Looking around, it's a simple, small home, well built with dark grey siding that blends well with the scenery.

"Would you like to come in? I could make us dinner if you haven't eaten yet today." I can tell he's slightly nervous with the way he says it.

I hesitate, not sure of what to say.

"It's okay. Sorry. I just thought if you haven't eaten, and I haven't…it's just better sometimes, not eating alone." His words hold a touch of hollowness.

"Why not?" Putting the car in park and shutting off the engine, I get out, following him to his home.

"I wasn't expecting company, so it's a little messy." Opening the door to his home, he waits for me to walk in first.

It's all open concept, everything in one room except the bedrooms and bathroom. It's clean, modern; the only thing out of place are some big medical books and a guitar on the couch. Some of the sun-ripened vegetables that I brought to the pack gathering are sitting on his table just waiting to be eaten.

"Come, sit." He pulls out a chair for me at the island. The gas range sits in the middle, high quality.

"Drinks." He says this to himself as he looks into the fridge.

"I have wine, beer, vodka, pop, water? Whatever you would like."

"I'll take a glass of wine."

He pulls a bottle of blushing pink wine out and pours two glasses. My fingertips brush against him as I take the glass from him. His eyes find mine before he looks away.

I notice his deck outside is bigger than his home, layered steps and landings that go all the way to the lake. He notices where my eyes are wandering.

"Would you like to go outside?" He opens the glass doors, letting the hot summer breeze in. Stepping outside, I see he has canoes, kayaks, and stand-up paddle boards that line the side of the deck.

"Wow, you have a lot of stuff."

"I like the water. Do you kayak?"

"No, I have never been." He looks surprised.

"I really was never invited, plus my parents don't live on the water. I always wanted to, but I just didn't have the opportunity."

"Well, if you want, I could teach you. Maybe if it's a nice weekend, you can come over in the afternoon and we can take a little tour of the lake." He's looking at the water, not at me. I can tell he's waiting for an answer.

"That would be fun, thanks." He lets out a breath with my words.

Sipping my wine, I look out at the lake shimmering in the afternoon sun.

"Beautiful," he says.

"It is," I agree, but when I look at him, he's looking at me.

CHAPTER 7

Almost

A light wind from the east pushes the water toward the shore. A loon calls its haunting song out as it drifts lazily in the hot summer sun. The retreat and advance of water leaves the sand on the beach wet one minute and dry the next. The bright rays beating down on my back has me wanting to jump into the cool water.

This week at work was good. I didn't have anything exciting happen. It allowed me to just concentrate on getting things where I like them. I haven't felt nor have I seen Clayton since that day. I feel good about that. Out of sight, out of mind. The Luna has even left me alone. On Friday, Dallas approached me to see if I was still interested in a canoe trip on Saturday, and at first, I said I was busy. His reply was that he "*understood.*" The way he said it was like he understood it had something to do with him. So I told him I would be there, and here we are.

There's a little island in the center of the lake that Dallas is taking us toward. We've been out canoeing for at least an hour, and my shoulders are burning with the effort. It doesn't look like it would be this hard, but it is.

"You okay?" he questions behind me. "You can stop paddling if you want."

"No, it's okay, I'm just not used to this," I reply, trying to push through the fire my arms are feeling.

"This is called Blueberry Island." He jumps out of the water, getting his shorts wet, pulling the canoe toward shore. He puts his hand out to steady me as I get out. When our hands meet, he looks away. I can't see his eyes because he's wearing sunglasses. It feels weird not being able to see wolves' eyes. They hold our soul.

I walk into the bushes, and the moss is so thick my feet sink down into the forest floor. Small wild blueberry plants line the sponge-soaked soil, carpeting it in specks of blue. These tiny morsels are so abundant and packed with the taste of deep summer.

Sitting down, gathering the blueberries up, I start gorging on the feast nature is providing. The coolness of the shade and the earth smooths out the mid-day heat.

"Here, take some of mine." He fills my hand full, watching me eat what he has just given me. He has a small smile gracing his face that makes him look *cute*.

He's in a short sleeve shirt that's loose against his chest, but when he moves, it becomes slightly tighter, showing off muscles hidden by the material.

His bicep flexes, peeking out his sleeve as he reaches and bends for more blueberries. Gazing at his forearms, I see something that makes me gasp.

Reaching out my fingertip, I trace the single line that runs from his inner wrist to his elbow. The scar is raised, more white than pink in color; it's old. Silver did it. He did this to himself…he meant his death when he did that; only the serious who think they want to meet the moon try to end their own life with that kind of cut. They don't understand that if you end your own life, you will never meet the moon.

"What did you do?" The question hangs in the air between us.

He looks down at his own arm, and his face takes on a solemn look.

"I'm surprised you haven't seen this before now." He doesn't try to hide it behind his back; instead, he traces the delicate line. "I was young. I just thought that ending my life was the solution I was looking for. I was wrong." He looks away from me as if remembering everything. "My mate, she died, and I thought that I just couldn't go on without her. I gave up." His voice shakes slightly, but he holds himself together.

"Sometimes I feel the same way, but I just can't do it." I let my confession leak out. I have never told anyone this. He takes his glasses off so I see those eyes of his that hold the color of a perfect blue sky.

"Don't ever think that. Promise me. He's not worth your life." His hands grab my arms, not roughly, just to hold me slightly.

"Please, if you ever feel that way, come to me." I nod my head at him, not trusting my voice at the moment.

"Look at me. He's not worth it."

"I know." His eyes hold mine for a moment, assessing me for the truth.

"I would never do anything like that, really. I've got my work now that I love. I've got my family. They have already been through enough."

"You should talk with Aurora. She's really good. I talk with her myself at times." He doesn't hide the fact that he needs someone to help him.

"I just started to. I think it's going to be good for me."

"It will, trust me." I still have his forearm in my hand. I can feel the heat his skin is giving off. His hand goes over mine with a little squeeze before he pulls himself away from my grasp. Putting his glasses back on, he stands, holding his hand out for me to take.

My chest almost brushes against him as he helps me stand. I can sense a shiver go through him. His eyes are hidden by his glasses. "We should go." That's all he says as he turns around, heading toward the canoe.

"So I invited some friends over. They should be there when we get back, if you don't mind. I thought, maybe, have a little get together, nothing formal. A bonfire, get the guitars out, some singing to the moon. Would you be interested in staying?"

"Yes, I would love to." Now it's my turn to smile. I feel slightly giddy; I always wanted to sit by a fire and listen to music.

The midday gets pushed to afternoon, and several wolves are here. The party becomes bigger and bigger with new additions coming every few minutes. *This is so nice*, I think, sipping on a drink.

"You're smiling. Are you having a good time?" Dallas has taken a break from hosting to talk with me.

"Actually, I am. This is the first time I have ever been to a party that wasn't a big pack get together. This is exactly how I pictured it would be. Thank you for the invite."

"First time at a party! That's really sad in a way, but at the same time I'm happy I could provide you with a first." He bows slightly to me. I bow back, taking another sip from the plastic cup.

"Rya!" Cora, with her young in her arms, waves to me.

"Hi, Cora. How are you?" She comes to stand with us.

"Dr. Valentine, thank you for inviting us out. I just love it here." She's looking out at the lake, taking in the beauty of the water.

"I made some burgers. I put them in your fridge. I couldn't find you." She eyes us but looks back to the lake.

"Thanks for doing that, but I told you just bring yourselves. I had everything taken care of."

She walks toward a shade tree. "I couldn't come empty handed. That's rude." Dropping the diaper bag on the grass, she's trying to spread out a blanket with one hand.

"Here, let me help you." Taking the blanket, I spread it out for her. The leaves of the big maple tree provides shelter from the burning sun on the delicate skin of the newborn.

She sits down cross-legged, putting her infant in her lap. She's sleeping contentedly, no idea she's at a party. We are sharing something in this minute, the baby and I, our first lake party.

"Well, I better get back to hosting. If you females need anything, just ask. I'm at *your* beck and call." He retreats back on the deck, where most of the crowd has gathered. Everyone is drinking their drinks, music is up, and voices are loud. Laughter, lots of laughing is going on. Some wolves are in the water, splashing around or using the toys that Dallas has spread out on the shore.

"This is so nice. I love it when Dr. Valentine throws these parties." She's scanning the crowd, looking at everyone here, then back to the lake.

"Maybe one day I might get a place out here." She has a longing in her voice, a want for a future she can picture in her mind.

Her mate comes to lay down beside her, kissing his little female's head, then his mate's neck. Taking in her scent, my stomach clenches slightly at my want for the future that can't happen.

"Hi, Rya," her male calls out.

"Hello, Mark, how are you?"

"Good." He really doesn't pay me any mind; his concentration is all in front of him. I watch as Cora's fingers play in his hair.

"Well, I should go. If you two want to go in the water or canoe, I could watch her for you, if you want."

Cora gets a giant smile on her face. "Really?

That would be great! I'll take you up on that offer, thanks."

"No problem." Turning from them, I watch as Dallas lights the fire in the pit at the lake's edge. The music is turned up; the wolves are in a party mood.

More and more wolves are showing up, and deep afternoon sets in, yet the wall of heat doesn't leave. Even in shorts and a tank top, my neck is sticky with sweat, fly away hairs sticking to my face.

The smell of barbecue wraps around the grounds, drifting hungrily in the air.

Dallas is entertaining the gathered, weaving in and out of the crowd. He's very social. In a way, I envy how easy it is for him to mingle.

Most of the females are in their bikinis in half stages of dryness. The lake is filling with people using it for their enjoyment. I contemplate taking off my clothes to take advantage of the cool water. Dallas is shirtless now, toned and tight. The clothes he wears at the office do not do justice to that male wolf.

Some of the lawn chairs are starting to make it to the fire pit. Guitars are starting to come out, being tuned slightly before variations of songs start to play out. I can't help but take it all in. Dallas comes over, holding a plate of food.

"Here, I brought you a plate. You haven't eaten yet." A variety of food, all in small portions, are spread neatly, nothing touching. He must not like his food touching.

"Thanks, I was going to make myself something soon. I was just waiting for everyone else to get something."

"You don't have to be last anymore. You should be eating first." He hands me the plate as well as the drink in his hand. It's homemade lemonade spiked with vodka, filled to the top with ice. In this heat, it won't take long for the ice to completely melt.

"Thanks, Dallas."

"Rya, are you still willing to watch her for us? We won't be long. I just fed her, and she should be out for a while," Cora says. She's dressed in a bikini, looking hopeful that I will say yes.

"Sure, you guys go. Take your time. I'll watch her." The little female is wrapped up in a blanket, laying on the blanket. Putting my plate and drink down, I cross my legs so she fits securely on my lap. I watch as they run toward the canoes. He grabs onto her ass, giving it a squeeze before her hand slaps his away. They're laughing together. I want that.

Taking a sip of my drink, I lean against the tree trunk. It's scratchy against my back. The little one is nestled against me, sleeping her day away. I feel him before I smell him. Hot eyes on me, caressing my skin with his stare. Putting my drink down so I don't drop it, I take in some calming breaths before I look his way.

What I see is him and Kennedy. She has her hand tracing his hipbone as she smiles at everyone. She waves happily to her friends. I want to pull my eyes away from the sight, but I can't.

I'm looking on hungrily, wanting to bite into their love. Her fingertips now trace the back of his neck. I look at her neck; it's no longer red or inflamed. It looks exactly like mine, unmarked.

He just stares at me. The tiny female in my lap wiggles for just a moment before settling back into dreams. I feel everywhere his eyes roam. Every single inch of skin he's looking at. I meet his eyes, then look away. His gaze falls off my body; the coolness that creeps in from the warmth I felt makes a shiver go through me. I look toward the lake. They are way out there, with no hope of them coming back soon. I prepare myself mentally. I need to get through this. I need to just start being able to be around them. I can't live my life hiding in fear that I bump into them. They are the future leaders of this pack, and it's inevitable that we will mingle together every now and then.

"I never invited them. Do you want me to ask them to leave?" Dallas is standing to the side of me, looking enraged. His face is red, and the veins in his arms are dilating, filling with blood.

"No, it's okay. I need to get used to this. Really, it's okay." Taking another sip of my drink, I don't think I can eat anymore, but maybe I can drink.

Dallas turns, walking toward them. Kennedy smiles at him, her bikini top overflowing with her female assets. I look down at my chest; it's just adequate compared to hers. She's tanned, toned, her nails a light pink, matching her lipstick. How one female can be so utterly beautiful is beyond me. Her face drops slightly while Dallas has a soft conversation with them, both nodding their heads his way.

Dallas walks away, then turns back around for a few more words. I see a twitch in Clayton's jaw, his lips tight. Kennedy has her hand still on his hip, thumb feeling flesh that belongs to *me.*

Some of the mated females make their way over to me, sitting down on the blanket, their backs turned toward the party looking at the lake. It's as if they are making a living wall of flesh to shelter me from the view of Clayton and Kennedy. Their voices are drowning out all the other voices in the crowd. Talking about nothing really, just trivial conversation to make noise.

I really don't know what to stay to these females who shunned me so badly in high school. It's like trying to swallow down bitterness. My smile is just not right. They are trying to be nice to me; I just can't forget what they have done to me.

"Rya, we need to say that we're sorry for the way we treated you. We never really knew what you had to go through until we found our mates. We want you to know that we're ashamed for what we put you through, and we're ashamed for what they are putting you through," one of the more vocal females of the group says. They give a disgusted look Kennedy's way; it's how I wish I could look at her, at them…but I don't.

"It's all right, we were all young. It's in the past, and I have moved on with my life. I can't say it's not difficult, because it is, but I'm going to be just fine. I have my work now, and I love what I'm doing." The half-truth spills out of my mouth for these females to drink up greedily.

All their shoulders relax with my words. I forgive them their youthful mistakes; I won't forget, but I can maybe forgive them. My resolve is switching back and forth, forgiveness or bitterness, a choice to make.

A hand goes on my shoulder, a hand on my leg, a hand on my other shoulder, light squeezes. A nuzzle to my cheek, they all take turns brushing against me slightly...the skin on skin contact that I have never had with a group of females before. It's slightly overwhelming, the acceptance they are showing me as if I'm part of the pack, a part of them.

His presence is getting closer. It's just a feeling, a sixth sense that I can feel without having to look at him. As they pass by us, he keeps his face staring straight ahead. Her fingers are in the band of his shorts, dipping down slightly.

Kennedy smiles toward us. "Hello, ladies," she says as she passes by. No words are returned her way. Her smile falters for just a second before she looks straight ahead at the lake without another word, passing the rest of the way in silence.

I watch them get into a paddle boat. They start making their way toward the little island that I was at earlier. I wonder if they are going to make love in the deep moss. I just can't help the picture my mind conjures.

Once they are far enough away on the lake, the females start getting up, walking away from me toward their own mates. They must be so thankful at this moment for what they have.

I'm glad when Cora finally gets back, relieving me of my babysitting duties.

"Thanks, Rya." She looks so beautiful at the moment, her hair still wet from a swim. I can smell love on her skin.

"No problem. If you ever need to get out, I can always watch her if I'm not busy." I press a small little kiss to the pup's forehead before handing her back to her mother. Walking away, I catch Dallas staring before he quickly looks away.

I refill my drink from the pitcher that sits on the table in the shade. The ice cubes are almost melted.

They still aren't back yet. The light is fading in the sky, and the fire lighting the beach area up. Guitar music is playing, and wolves are swaying in their chairs. Dallas has his guitar in his hands as he motions for me to come and sit at the fire. I take an empty seat just a few seats down from him. Noticing the way the fireflies start to flicker on and off, I try to predict when I might see where they might pop out next.

Rhythmic pedaling getting closer to the shore alerts me to steel my nerves for their approach. Putting my hands underneath my thighs, I hold myself down. The blue base is just above the water. She gets out, dressed only in her wet bikini and slightly damp hair. I avoid looking at him in fear that he can feel my gaze on his body. They take a seat at the fire with all of us.

"Clay, did you bring your guitar?" one of the wolves questions him.

"No." That's all he says, his gaze on my body again. I try to angle away from him.

It takes everything I have not to look at them. Instead, I watch Dallas start to strum his guitar. He smiles softly at me. Fingers running along the steel strands, mournful music coming out the wooden belly. He makes the guitar sing. I just can't help but be hypnotized by the poetry. Firelight dances in his eyes. It's a moment we're sharing before a very low growl tumbles into the night. The music of the guitars barely covers it up.

"I should go. Thanks for today, Dallas. I appreciate it so much. You have no idea." Giving everyone at the fire a little wave goodbye, I turn, walking away.

"Wait, I'll walk you to your car." We stroll side by side in silence until we reach the car.

"Really, Dallas, thank you for today. It's the most fun I've had in a really long time." He steps slightly closer to me as I fumble with my keys.

"Anytime. You're welcome here anytime." He's not looking away this time. He's holding his ground. A fingertip touches the side of my face. It slides against my jawline. I lean into it slightly, and his other hand goes on the curve of my hip, pulling me toward him. Our bodies are flush; everything is touching. Slowly, he inches closer to me, giving me time to pull away if I want to. His lips are so close to mine, so close, before I pull away from him. Feeling heat against my back, I can feel him watching this moment, this first moment I almost had.

"That was…I'm sorry, Rya." His hand runs over his shaved head.

"I have to go." I'm flustered, red-faced, breathing hard, heart hammering in my chest.

"That was stupid of me."

"It's okay. I need to go." I close the door. I need to leave now.

74

He's looking down at the ground, upset with himself. All I can feel are eyes burning into me as I drive away. They don't leave me, not until I'm far away from his sight.

CHAPTER 8

Imposters

Summer is now falling into autumn. I like how my dad's in his flannel shirt, a rake in his hand, burning the dry leaves in my fire pit by the lake that he helped me build. White smoke curls around in the wind, shrouding the nearby woods with its opaque veil.

My mother helps with all the canning, collecting the harvest that another wolf left in the earth for me to reap in mason jars that line my counter, all warm and cooling. *Such a bounty*, I think. Mother Nature has so much to offer as I drink my warm pumpkin tea. That old wolf's smell is almost gone from my home, just the faintest trace that she was ever here before me. I just like the thought of something just belonging to me.

A kiss to my shoulder has me smiling at my mother. She presses her cheek to my face, smelling me into her before pulling away.

"Thanks again, Mom, for helping me. I

appreciate it so much. I couldn't have done it myself." So much work, it took all afternoon yesterday just to pick and wash all the tomatoes.

"I think that I'm enjoying it more than you, Rya." My whole family is becoming closer, healing slowly from the poison that so ruined us.

"Dad, you should start the barbecue. They should be here soon." My sisters and their mates are coming to celebrate my birthday. This will be my first family dinner at my home.

I clean up the kitchen, making sure that everything is tidy, and put out some wine like grownups do. We are all grown wolves now.

Throughout the day, I can feel eyes on me. I can feel him watching me with my family at times then leaving, coming back…I can't smell him, the wind is the wrong direction, but I can feel him. The hair on my arms stand on end at times.

I don't acknowledge his eyes, refusing to let him know that I feel him on me.

My older sister arrives with her mate, a homemade birthday cake in her hands, vanilla with cherry chip icing.

My middle sister arrives next with bags of presents that her mate carries in his hands. All greet me with cheek pressed against cheek. Their smells mingle with the steaks that are now grilling.

They all take places at my table, filling it with their smiling faces, pouring wine into the glasses. Everyone is in good spirits. I can't stop the happiness from pouring out of me. I wonder if they can smell it.

The old wooden table holds the summer bounty

full of grilled vegetables my garden provided.

As we take our seats, I hear a car pull into my driveway, footsteps crushing on the gravel, getting closer, then gradually getting further away, as if someone changed their minds. Getting up, I go to the front door and look out. Dallas is just opening his car door, getting in.

"Dallas," I call to him. He looks my way.

"I saw the smoke from my side of the lake. I thought you might want some company. I didn't want to disturb you. I'll see you Monday," he calls out from his car.

"No, you're not disturbing anything. We were just going to eat. I have so much food. Come eat with us." He hesitates, teeter tottering on a decision.

"Come on, we have steak," I say, trying to entice him to stay.

"My family won't bite." Taking a breath in, he closes his door before walking toward me.

"Come around back."

My father and mother exchange glances with one another before they busy themselves with cutting the meat on their plates. I set another place at the table, just for him.

Dallas pauses at the screen door before coming inside. He's looking at my family, unsure if he really should be here.

"Dallas, come in, sit down. Help yourself! Would you like some wine to drink, or I have beer?" He looks around at what everyone else's glasses are filled with.

"I'll take some wine, thanks."

"Dr. Valentine, how are you?" My mother's

voice is pleasant on the ears, welcoming a strange wolf into our meal.

"Good, thank you." He keeps his voice very polite toward her.

"Dr. Valentine—"

"Please, sir, call me Dallas."

"All right, Dallas. What brings you here?" my father asks sternly.

"Dad!" My voice raises in embarrassment.

"I just saw the smoke from her fire. I live across the lake, so I thought I would just stop by and say hi." He looks at my father, holding his eye.

"Those leaves were giving off a lot of smoke." I look toward the fire pit. It's smoldering with just the faintest wisp of smoke spiraling toward the waning sunlight. An uncomfortable silence follows.

My sister and her mate stand up, holding hands, smiling at each other. "We have an announcement to make." He kisses her hand.

"We're going to have a pup." I knew she went into her heat, but I didn't want to ask because the last few times weren't very successful.

Getting out of my chair, I hug her to me. "I am so happy for you." My mother starts crying—her first grandchild. Even my father's eyes are watering. Everyone sheds happy tears, grateful tears. I send a prayer of thanks to the moon. They have been trying for years and years.

Dallas is sitting there looking slightly uncomfortable, but maintaining appearances.

Once the excitement has calmed down, plates are cleared into the sink. Fresh tea is put out with dessert plates.

My mother goes to the fridge and pulls out my cake. I can't help the stupid smile that spreads wide across my face. Nothing is better than this: my family happy, enjoying themselves. It's like the past never happened and the future is just so full of hope.

"Happy birthday, Rya." Excited, everyone is cheering. Dallas looks at me in question but says nothing.

All of them join singing happy birthday to me. This is the first time I have someone other than my family sing happy birthday to me since I shifted. His voice is masculine and deep against my ears. Mom places the cake in front of me with all twenty-three candles lit. Looking out the window, I see him, just the shadow of him watching us...my family celebrating another year of my life. Their voices are raised loudly, so I know he hears. He knows it's my special day, yet he's not sitting at my table with me.

"Make a wish." I look at everyone's expectant faces and wish for my own *happiness*. I'm selfish, but that's what I ask for.

I blow out the candles in one go. Dallas leans toward my ear and whispers, "You should have told me it was your birthday."

"It's not a big deal." I glance at him with a shrug of my shoulder.

"You're wrong! It is a big deal." He pulls his mouth away from my ear. I need to get up to cut the cake.

Handing my family slices of cake, I ask, "Dallas, would you like a piece?"

Eyes of Caribbean blue sea bore into me. "Yes, I'd like a piece." I hand him the plate, and he takes it, letting his fingers touch mine. We make eye contact just a moment longer than it should, and it's my turn to start blushing. He notices while I try to look some place other than his eyes.

He's growing out his hair. I can almost fist it with my hand and pull his mouth on mine if I *wanted* to. He's starting to cloud my mind. It's unfamiliar to me, thinking about this male wolf who *almost* kissed me. I can still sense the way his lips *almost* brushed against mine. That thought sends such images inside me, fantasizing about his lips on mine. Instead of all my night time dreaming of Clayton, Dallas is now stalking his way inside my thoughts. Even my daytime thoughts are starting to include him.

The tension between the two of us is like a string, pulling tight at the ends, ready to snap at any minute. It's taunting us, having a good laugh on our behalf.

At work, we try to pretend it doesn't exist. I can see it in his eyes when he looks at me, looking at my lips. I have to pretend I don't notice the wolf's eyes that have a dominance now in his stare. He tries his best to suppress his nature, at times having to leave the room flushed with an excuse of needing to check something in his office. Nothing has happened between us since that night.

I can see the way his head turns, mouth slightly parting in an easy smile. It gives me feelings deep down in my stomach that makes me want to reach out and touch him.

Even though my stomach is full, I hunger for something else. My chest rumbles inside; it's sudden, without warning. I look back up; his eyes haven't left mine. The table is hushed. I'm mortified now. Getting up, I go to the sink and start to do the dishes.

"I'm sorry," I mumble to everyone.

It's like I'm so malnourished from being so alone for so long, he has something that can satisfy me. I want to let myself indulge in him...

My father gets up, grumbling that he needs some air. Dallas is right behind him. The mates of my sisters practically run out. I can see them through the kitchen window, standing by the fire. Dallas, with his hands by his side, eyes my father, my sisters' mates surrounding him. Shoulder back, head held high. I try to turn my ears their way to listen in on what they're saying to each other.

My father looks at the lake, nods his head yes, wiping away at his eye. A long discussion with hand gestures and posturing toward Dallas. He holds himself still, listening as they all give him something that's on their minds. Dallas nods in agreement with everything they say.

"How long have you been interested in him?" Her voice hits my back with my sisters standing behind her.

"I'm not."

"Don't lie. We always can tell when you're lying. We just let you believe that we're tricked by your words." That takes my breath away with her truth.

"I just think that he's nice." The plate in my hand

almost falls back into the soapy water.

"Has he met his mate yet?" There was a hint of sadness in her voice.

"She died." They all inhale a breath.

"So he's free to be claimed."

"Mother, I have a mate."

"Who doesn't want you." It's spit out by my sister. Her disgust for him rolls off her body in powerful waves of contempt.

Looking out the window, I can see that my father is shaking hands with Dallas, along with my sisters' mates. Giant grins are on all their faces.

"What pack is he from?"

"I never asked. All I know is that his mate died and he's here. That's it. I don't want to talk about this again." Turning to look at my mother, I let her know this conversation is over.

My mother goes to open her mouth again. "Stop, Mom."

The males enter the house, Dallas giving me a once-over before looking away.

"Time for presents!" my sister cheers.

Bags are placed in front of me, and everyone watches as I open gifts bought with love. Each one has a special meaning to the buy. I feel overwhelmed with emotion. I don't need the presents; I just need this. How it is right now, in this moment...this is the best feeling.

Dallas sits close to me on the couch, not touching, just there beside me. I can feel the heat of him soaking into my skin, and a shiver passes through me. This is how Clayton must feel with Kennedy beside him. This is how he must constantly feel by her presence, a constant state of arousal.

My family stays well into the night, laughing and telling Dallas stories of when I was a small pup. My mother tells him I was born in the month of abundance, that I'm a giver, always giving what I had to others. It starts with a yawn by my father, stating he needs to get to bed, that he's too old to stay up so late. My sisters follow, leaving Dallas, who doesn't look too keen to go anywhere except where he's sitting.

My stomach is fluttering to be all alone with this male wolf.

"Do you want anything else to drink or eat?" I'm at the sink, putting away the dry dishes.

"No, I'm fine." His voice has dropped lower. He's standing right behind me now. I hold onto the sink with my hands to steady myself. I can feel him taking the hair tie that binds my braid. He doesn't say a word. His nose rests against my head, inhaling. He unravels my hair; it's loose, wavy. His fingers start to run through it. This is the first time a male has groomed me. Strong fingers run through the pale blond hair; my scalp is tingling.

His warm breath tickles behind my ear, then the softest kiss is placed on my neck. The collar of my red shirt is pulled to expose the skin of my shoulder. He tastes me with his tongue. My legs are going to give out; I can feel it.

"Rya." His hand on my hip turns me to face him.

It's slow motion glorious the way he steps into me...the way his male body brings quivers to my skin. Soft lips brush against my cheekbone, a nip to my jawline. I can feel his head pull away just enough for our eyes to meet. He doesn't let me have time to decide; he decides for me. His lips are gentle against mine. A hint of tongue glides out against my mouth. I move my mouth with his lead, hands wrapping around his neck, pulling myself into him. A rumble deep inside of him shakes me. I'm shaking.

I can't get close enough as I rub against the part that makes me quiver. He gives a moan, biting softly on my bottom lip. I can smell myself, my body's response to drive him forward, signaling to the wolf that I am receptive to his advances.

A hand that was on my hip slips inside my shirt, and his palm, so smooth, traces my ribs resting just under my bra line. I moan into him; this feels beyond what I ever thought possible.

Lips against lips, his tongue tasting mine, hand running down my spine, feeling every vertebra. Cupping my ass, he presses himself into me. His other hand is at the base of my neck, my hair tangling in his fingers.

He's sweet, soft velvet.

It's a divine seduction as he woos me with pleasure. He's treating me like artwork that he's painting with his body, his mouth, his tongue. He's trembling, lips now against my neck, inhaling deeply. I'm so aroused, my open desire for him pulsing in heavy rhythms along all my nerve endings. I'm aching for something more, some deep need that hasn't been sated yet. My hands have made their way inside his shirt. Claws have come out against his back, lining them with my marks…

My head angles back as he scrapes his teeth against virgin flesh. He is unleashing my chaos.

I'm in chaos.

His mouth captures my moans in his, the friction of him rubbing into my core leaving me panting. I'm memorized in a bliss-rush. My boundaries are blurring...

Pulling himself away from me slightly, he says, "I should go." We take this second to breathe in fully before he's on me again, taking my self-control with every nip of his mouth.

An erotic battle, his claws are out, gripping me firmly to him so I can't move. His mouth sucks on my skin, pulling it into him. My eyes are closed as he picks me up. He carries me somewhere; I don't care where we go as long as he doesn't stop the feeling he's giving me. Laying me on my bed, he positions himself between my parted legs and begins to rub up against me, stimulating something deep inside.

"Dallas." I moan out his name, and his lips are there to swallow his name down inside of him. My shirt rises on my body; his shirt is off. Did I take it off?

He's looking down at me. My bra is exposed for his eyes. The only male wolf that has ever wanted to see my flesh.

His chest heaves up and down, and his tongue traces where bra meets flesh. My heels dig into the back of his legs to put more weight against my center. His hips rock into me, up and down, impossibly slow. His muscles down his stomach clench and flex with each breath, with each roll of his hips.

He's back on my mouth, kissing harder with more of a need male wolves have. Teeth scrape against my neck, lingering over where a mark can be placed.

"I should go." He's saying this yet still kissing me. My thighs are squeezed around him, not letting him move away. He's tasting every curve of my breast without going into the fabric of my tiny bra. Teeth bite softly at the hardened peaks, driving me insane for more. I want more than what I should have. My back arches, pressing more of my chest into his mouth, demanding more, moaning out for the night air to take my lust up to the moon.

"I need to leave." His resolve wins out as he gets up, putting his shirt back on. With his hand, he helps me up.

"Happy birthday, Rya." His lips brush against my lips again. I try to pull him back on the bed, but he's unmovable.

"You make it difficult to stop." He kisses my eyelids, both my cheeks. He places a lingering kiss to the place that can only bear one wolf's mark.

Walking him to the door, I feel lust drunk and giggly, swooning over the male in front of me.

"Lock the door behind me, Rya."

"Why?" I reply, breathless.

"So I can't get in." A quick kiss is placed against my lips before he leaves. I lock the door behind him, thinking, could Dallas be my *imposter*, my *fake*…my *fraud?*

CHAPTER 9

Fork Tongue Road

Twirling.

That's how I feel. Like I can spin around in circles singing to the moon in thanks and praise for this change, this new beginning for me. I even have the music on this morning getting ready for work. It's as if every musical note is absorbing in my body as I sing along to the song.

This is another first for me. Usually, I don't get as involved in singing as I do my makeup. Just a hint of eyeshadow to maybe bring out my eyes more. A very light tinge of red lip gloss. I kiss the mirror, leaving behind an imprint of my lips.

Looking at the mirror, the person staring back at me has brighter eyes, like a snake shedding its old, faded skin. My face looks like it's glowing and pink. The fake smile that always looks back at me is now being replaced by my heart's smile.

I feel so good.

My face keeps getting redder and redder with the

thoughts of him and that kiss, that first kiss that will be with me for my lifetime.

He's like my own personal sun, warming me from the inside out. I twirl again inside my home, whose smell is almost my own.

My heart skips a beat just thinking about him. He might really like me. Maybe I might have a chance. Just that dim ray of hope has me giddy with excitement. I tried to call him yesterday to see if he wanted to hang out or anything. He didn't answer his phone, so I was forced to leave an awkward message, which made me embarrassed. I didn't want to come off sounding too eager, but I just couldn't help it.

I'm actually so nervous to go to work today and see him. I need to try to calm myself or else everyone will be able to smell my excitement if I let my emotions get the best of me.

Walking to work, I have to restrain myself not to skip down the road.

I look in at everyone's yards. Neat piles of leaves dot the grass, evidence that they just couldn't get all the yard work done in one weekend. Soon I will be smelling the whiff of frost on the earth. The trees are starting to look lonesome with the dropping of their leaves, leaving behind a carpet mosaic of crimsons, oranges, and yellows.

Today, the sunrise is blood red in the sky. Such beauty in nature, all you have to do is look. The days are shortening, and the nights will start to get colder. I can't wait to light my fireplace when the snow starts to fall.

Taking a deep breath before walking in, I try to

act cool. Like I always fix my hair for work and wear makeup. Looking around, I can see a light on in his office. Aurora isn't here yet.

I knock softly on his office door, and my heart beats wildly in my chest.

"Come in."

When I look at him, I give him my best heart smile; it's from my soul. It's true and without restraint.

What greets my eyes isn't his smile. Instead, he has fading bruises. His throat is torn up, as if another wolf was trying to tear it out.

"Rya, sit down." I take a seat directly across from his desk, hands in my lap or else they will try to touch him. He's not giving out any signals that he wants me to touch him.

"What happened?" My heart is starting to sink.

"A disagreement." That's all he says before a quiet takes hold.

Sighing to himself, he seems as if he wants to say something but doesn't know where to begin.

He's looking into my eyes, which are full of concern.

"What happened, Dallas?" Standing, I try to touch his face, but he flinches away. My hand goes to my side before I sit back down.

I'm holding my breath for some reason, as if I'm waiting for something bad to come out of his mouth. The bottom of my stomach starts to choke. A small breath catches in my throat as I bite my bottom lip with his extended silence.

"Are you hurt?" I try looking for more than cuts and bruises.

"No!"

"I'm sorry." For some reason, I feel the need to apologize, but I'm not sure why.

"You have nothing to be sorry for. This was my—I came to you." His eyes close slightly, jaw twitching in tension.

"What happened?"

"Your mate doesn't like what belongs to him being *touched*." His voice is even, hands folded on his desk. His shoulders are tense. Maybe a flash of teeth is shown for just a second before he reins himself back.

"He has someone else. I'm—" He stops me from saying anything else.

"He's your mate. I thought I could fool myself, that something so good could come along, that I could be blessed again. I was wrong. You have someone for you, and I would just be your Kennedy." He's not looking at me. He's holding onto his hands in a vise grip.

"What happens to me, Rya, in the end? What would happen to me? I don't think I can take another heartbreak. It would kill me." He looks vulnerable, trying to expose feelings that are making him hurt from the inside.

"He doesn't want me." I say it with certainty from all these years of being alone.

"He's an Alpha male whose mate is being sniffed at by another male intent to take what belongs to him. He doesn't need to love you. His nature demands that he fight for you."

"Oh." I let that one word hang in the air as I try to control my trembling chin. My diaphragm expands with the long intake of air. I breathe it out slowly. The pull in of breath, the push out of breath, I know this feeling…*just breathe.*

"I thought I could do this. I was wrong. At least it was only a kiss that we shared, nothing too serious." He's looking down at his desk now. *Only a kiss.* He says it like it was only a kiss to him. To me, it was everything that I dreamed about.

"I think it would be best if we just kept our relationship on a professional level from now on." He's using his doctor's voice on me while I try to not cry. The tears want to pool in my eyes, but I am just trying to fight it the best I can.

"Is this what you want, Dr. Valentine?" Holding my breath until my head starts to feel dizzy, I wait for his answer.

"I think that would be best." He's not looking at me. He's looking at some stupid picture on his wall that's taking his attention away from my torn heart.

Getting off the chair slowly so I don't fall, I turn my back to him. It remains straight, no shoulders hunching forward. I will not look defeated in front of this male.

"I respect your choice." Turning the handle, I let myself out, closing the door quietly behind me. I make it to my office before the first tear slips out, and the others follow close behind.

"I wish this could be different," he says, emotionless behind me after the door closes. It's faint, but I can hear it.

Sitting behind my desk, I focus on the things that I need to be thankful for: my family, my career, my life. I could be dead, and that would be it. Try to focus on the positive.

I manage to get through my day, keeping my door closed after my females leave. I stay closed up inside until I know he has left for the day. That's when I emerge slowly, dragging my feet.

The walk home takes double the time that it took me this morning.

Walking into my room, I lay down on my bed, letting my pillowcase soak up all my sorrow.

My tears sanitize my clouding mind, cleansing my soul.

Crying is not a bad thing, as Aurora says, so when you have that need to cry...*cry.*

The floodgates to my heart are open, and screams of frustration are muffled by my pillow. Once nothing is left, rage starts creeping in on its hands and knees, slowly slithering inside of me.

How dare he! All these years of suffering just to come back here and find something small and maybe special, and he has to ruin it. This is how obituaries are made.

The car ride is quick to his home, faster than I have driven in a long time.

I pound on the pack house door. My fist seems like it could go clear through if I let it.

Luna Catherine opens the door, regarding me up and down with an apple in her hand. A sly smile is on her face.

"Where is your son?" My voice shakes in fury, my madness hardly contained. I feel like a tornado twisting on an irrational path ready to tear up this place.

Her teeth flash in warning to settle down.

"He's out back speaking with Kennedy." She smiles a wolf's smile, and I have to look closely to see if her tongue is forked behind the canines that flash. She takes a bite of her apple, and its crispness makes a crunching sound, a small spray of juice squirting out. I feel such darkness overcoming me that, in a fleeting thought, I think I can take the Luna on. A low rumble tumbles out of her chest as if she can read my mind.

She opens the door wider for me to come into their den. Not her office, she leads me into their personal space, where usually no pack members get to go.

Kimberly is curled up on the couch, sleeping like a little girl taking a nap after a busy morning. She looks so peaceful. Part of me wants to be quiet so she can get the rest that her body needs to incubate a life.

I look around at the walls. They are filled with family pictures of all of them.

A small picture sits on the coffee table of Clayton and Kennedy smiling into the camera, faces all muddy, toothless in bathing suits, playing in a puddle. A moment captured by a mother who thought how adorable they are.

The fireplace mantle is covered in memories. I have no place in this life. I can't help but stare at everything. His life has no space for me.

She brings me to the window that looks out over the back lawn. I see them there by the apple tree; she's crying in his arms, her body shaking so fiercely with sobs that he needs to hold her to his chest. His lips are on her head, his hands trying to

94

wipe away the tears. He tries to push her slightly away from him, only for her to grab onto his shirt, pulling herself back into him. She's telling him something, fists on his chest pounding at him.

I feel like I could break her fingers so she couldn't touch what belongs to me. In this moment, my rage leaves with that thought. Dallas is *right*. He would be my lie if I can't stop thinking that Clayton belongs to me. I wish I could stop my hands from shaking when I see them together.

Another crunch from the apple turns my head the Luna's way. She's standing beside me watching the show, eating her apple. I hope she bites into a big fat worm so she can taste foulness on her tongue instead of the happiness I'm smelling from what she's seeing.

Kennedy's falling down now on her knees, holding onto his legs, her head bowed, pressing against his shins, words tumbling out of her mouth that I can't hear. His hand is on her head, running through her hair, trying to calm her with touch.

His eyes are closed, his chest heaving up and down. Bruises are all over his face, and his neck looks like someone went for a kill and missed just slightly. It's healing well. Within a day, it should be gone, like the fight between two males never happened.

Emerald orbs focus entirely on me, lighting my skin on fire, his dirty blond hair messy in the front, as if he were trying to pull his own hair out. His eyes are red and puffy; they match my own.

I'm looking like some gawker at a horrible car crash scene. I just can't look away. This is a very private moment between the two of them, and I am witnessing it.

She's pounding the ground at his feet. The creature is completely broken. He takes a position to stand in front of her, shielding her from our view. Protecting her from our intrusive eyes. He sinks down on his knees, picking her up like a newborn. A gentle rocking as her head lays against his chest. Rotten apples in various stages of decay litter the ground. Can they smell the rot that's festering around them?

"I want a transfer out." I still can't let my eyes leave them, standing shoulder to shoulder with the Luna.

"No, we won't grant you a transfer. You're ours, and we won't give you away to another pack." She takes another bite of the apple. How sweet is it on her tongue, the apple or the present circumstances?

"I won't stay."

"You will stay. There's nowhere for you to go." A faint hint of sadness is in her voice. "This is where you belong."

He's still rocking her, cooing into her ear. He smoothes her hair down, his back still turned our way.

"This is your chance, Rya. You need to take it. Fight for him." She's trying to offer me advice that I don't want.

"I tried to fight for him once. I have the scars to prove it." It's then that Kennedy's head lifts up, and our eyes connect. She looks exactly how I looked all those years ago. Pulling away from his grip, she stands to take a step toward the house. She staggers slightly before righting herself. Canines descending, claws coming out of her fingertips, her rage is potently directed at me. The darkness is swirling in those black irises. Her resolve is to take out the competition.

I can hear her yelling now, her voice raised in anger.

"How dare she come to *our home*!" She's looking at me like *I'm* the other female. That I came knocking on their door to destroy her world.

In this moment, I do feel like the other woman, his dirty little secret that's just coming out now. Except everyone has always known I am his *except them*.

With each step, skin is giving way to fur. The hair along the ridge of her spine is raised, hackles up. She's stiff legged, posturing jaws snapping open and shut. Teeth bared, waiting to sink into my flesh. She's issuing a challenge to me. My nature is gripping me, wanting to tear into the throat of life, spill her blood once and for all, get rid of my competition, this complication.

Clayton looks on. A hand grips the scruff of her neck as she tries to clamp onto his hand with sharp teeth. Her wolf is insane with a need to fight. He's restraining her in a tight grip. His body wraps around her dense form, trying to subdue the wolf. Places are switching. It's his turn now to restrain his moon from his mate.

"Leave," he says to me, looking straight in my eyes. "You shouldn't be here." His words hold disgust, as if I'm the catalyst for everything that I'm witnessing. That I am to blame for all this. He looks at me with such outward contempt that I take a step back. In this moment, all I can see is pure, unfiltered loathing from the both of them.

Breathe.

"Leave now!" Kimberly is stirring awake on the couch, eyes opening lazily, a stretch so her little belly sticks out of her shirt. She has a confused look in her eyes that I am in their home.

I look around at everything in this room. My pictures would never feel right in a room that belongs to them. I would never really be able to get her smell out of this place. Out of him.

The wolf that Clayton holds tries to break free, to fight for what she wants. Agony is on his face. She's in his bones, he might not be able to hold her mark, but she has branded his soul. They have greedily invaded and gorged themselves full on their love for each other. The legacy that they are making is a forked tongue trail. They have no one to blame but themselves.

She can have him.

He's not worth my fight.

CHAPTER 10

Let The Pain Begin

The first north wind started up late last night, screaming its way through the trees. It has brought a slight frost to the area this morning that should be melted soon. The wind is cold, blowing up my sleeves and nipping at my skin. Outside, the trees sway in a certain rhythm with the gusts of air. Maybe tonight I might have my first fire in my house. I think I will celebrate and get takc out for the occasion.

Starting a little later today than usual, I walk into the clinic. Aurora is there, and the place is packed, filled with mothers and their sick pups: runny noses, coughs, sore throats, and ears. All the little ones look miserable as they lay their heads on their parents' laps or shoulders, coughing and whining.

Dr. Valentine will be busy for most of the day; those poor pups are so susceptible to infections. They are just like human children until they shift. That's why the packs will fight for physicians and recruit them with massive incentives and perks. I wonder what they offered him to come here?

At least these last five days have been quiet with everyone leaving me alone. Not even the lurker made an appearance to my home. He kept away, probably to provide comfort and care to his moon. The thought disturbs me, but it is not as bad as it used to be. I can deal with it much better. I can maybe really for once in all these years just shrug the feeling off.

I can tell Dr. Valentine is in one of the small clinic rooms from the muffled voice behind the door. His smile is still contagious even though it's not turned my way. I catch him out of the side of my eye, laughing as he comes out of a room with a small pup, whose eyes look all glassy and cheeks of red fire. He has his hand on the mother's shoulder, smiling at her about something. I just stand there watching for just a second too long before his eyes find mine. Every time he catches me watching him, I feel he must think I'm stalkerish.

"Good morning, Rya." Our dialogue is kept painfully simple.

"Good morning, Dr. Valentine." He goes into another small room where a patient is waiting for him, not even pausing for the words to come out of my mouth.

It's like he closed the curtains on us, the production that barely even started. Our story just stopped before it really had a chance to begin.

Putting my bag down on my desk, I take a seat. My cheeks are flushed from seeing him; I'm still so very fond of his face. I just can't shut my emotions off. Even though he told me that we should keep it professional, I just can't help fantasizing about him and that kiss.

Friday, everyone is excited for the weekend, and I decided that I'm painting my bedroom. The color? Agreeable grey. The lady at the paint shop convinced me to buy it. I also bought this beautiful duvet. It's really a big fluffy cloud, a cocoon I don't want to get out of in the morning. The cover for it is pomegranate red; the lady at the bedding store said it suited me.

My Friday is a very quick half day; Dr. Valentine's in and out of rooms. I keep my door open. I can't resist attempting to catch glimpses of his face. I can see the lines in his forehead, how he gives the prescriptions to the mothers. The stubble on his jaw from at least six days' worth of growth, the slant of his shoulders, the way the top button on his collar is undone because it's becoming too tight around his neck. For the smallest fraction of a second, I can see his eyes as they touch mine before he turns away.

My last appointment is Kimberly, who's chewing gum, looking like such a small juvenile. No older than me when I first shifted. She still doesn't have her adult features yet. Her hips are still so narrow; she needs more meat on her bones. This is going to be extremely hard on her.

"Come in, Kimberly." I smile easily to her, not showing any teeth, trying to calm her nerves down. I put my hand on her shoulder, a little rub of comfort.

The door to the clinic opens, and Clayton walks

in. He's looking right at me. He takes my breath away...he will always take my breath away. It's what the moon wants, and he will always do that to me.

Quickly leading her into the examining room, I shut the door tight.

"Sorry about him coming. My mom's gone with Kennedy, and Dad had this meeting this morning. I don't drive yet, so he brought me." She's staring at the pictures I have put up with those newborn faces.

"That's all right, Kimberly. Nothing to apologize for." I try my best to sound believable.

"Let's have a look at you, shall we?" She climbs up on the table, pulling her shirt up to expose the slight protrusion of her belly. Her hand naturally starts to rub her tummy as all future mothers do. Taking her measurements, I notice that she's falling shy of what should be her normal progression. With such a young age, this is the first warning sign that something is off.

"Kimberly, are you eating at least five meals a day?"

She looks away from me, guilty. "Yes."

"Lie! Don't lie to me, Kimberly." Looking right in her eyes, I demand the truth. She sucks in a breath, staring at my eyes. Her hand goes up to touch my face. "Your eyes." That's all she says before placing her hand to her sides. She looks embarrassed she touched me.

"No. I don't want to get fat." I close my eyes, shaking my head.

"You need to eat. You need to put on weight so your pup grows strong. He can't grow if you don't eat." Her shoulders hunch forward.

Helping her off the exam table, I bring her into my office.

"Do you mind coming into the office for just a moment?" I avoid his eyes. This has to stop. She needs food or else she and her pup's lives will be endangered. No matter what I think of her brother, I have a duty to do. I notice Dr. Valentine's office door is wide open.

Clayton walks in, breathing through his mouth. He sits close to his sister, who's looking like she's in trouble. His arm goes around her shoulder with a little rub and a ruffle of her hair.

"Don't do that, Clay. You're messing up my hair." He gives her a smile, a real beautiful, brotherly smile that does things to my body.

I can see him looking around at my pictures on the wall, of the newborns with me holding them.

"Clayton." His hand grips onto the armrest. I think I hear it crack with the force. I can see hair starting to come on his forearms. He gets up off his chair, turning his back on the both of us, his hand on the door as if he's trying to turn it open, but his claws are starting to descend, making it impossible. He's trying to breathe through his mouth, big chest heaving, mind-cleansing breaths.

I need to say something for him to get control of himself. I think my mouth is open slightly, along with Kimberly's at the moment. It's rare for full-grown males to fight skin against fur.

"Your sister hasn't been eating properly since Luna Catherine is gone. Someone needs to keep an eye on her. She needs to eat at least five times a day. She needs good food, natural food." Kimberly's head hangs low, shoulders hunched. If she were in wolf form, her tail would be between her legs.

"Kim, why haven't you been eating?" His words are muffled slightly, and his whole body turns toward her in concern. His attention is only on her. His shift is stopping.

"I didn't want to get fat. If I get fat, then he won't like me anymore. He'll reject me for someone else." Big fat tears start trailing down her face. I get a tissue for her, coming to stand in front of her. I get down on my knees so we are both equals in this room. His warm breath is hitting the side of my face; my skin goosebumps naturally.

"Your mate won't think you're getting fat. He will think how beautiful you are. How healthy you look." She's crying now, great body moving sobs.

"I'm just so afraid that my mate will reject me like my brother rejected you." I watch as Clayton closes his eyes for a fraction of a second before focusing them on Kimberly.

"Kimberly, it's different between Clayton and me. You know that. It's not the same as your situation." I'm gently rubbing her back as she wipes her nose on the tissue.

"Kim, is that what you think?" She nods her head yes. A very unpleasant quiet takes hold in the office. It's only disturbed by her trying to calm her crying. I can't look up at Clayton, though I can feel his eyes on me. I can feel them on the side of my face, my neck at the spot that should have been claimed by now. I can feel them sweep over my lips, my hair, down my spine inch by inch until his gaze is pulled away.

"Kim." Her name is spoken so softly, I can't believe it could come out of his mouth. He puts both hands on her shoulders. "Look at me, Kimberly." Her deer eyes look up at her big brother.

"Rya." He says my name, and his whole body shudders. He drops to his knees in front of us. His mouth extends into that of a wolf, his head shaking from side to side.

"Stop." It's a garbled sound, a flagrant growl sounds from his chest. His hands are fists, knuckles pushing into the floor. His claws are starting to break skin, causing a small puddling of blood to leak out.

"Holy shit!" Kimberly jumps up, looking at her brother losing his mind on my office floor. The wolf's eyes stare back at Kimberly. Black orbs devoid of any color, the wolf pushing himself forward hard...a snap of the jaw Kimberly's way has me stepping in front of her, protecting the female from this unstable male.

His head comes up, nose sniffing the air. Body crouched on the ground, the fur and skin side in a state of anarchy.

He's agile, standing on two legs instead of four, his shift in stasis. Neither side is able to win.

We stay like this for just a minute before he finally gets the upper hand on that wolf of his.

"Clayton, what just happened?" Kimberly sounds as confused as I feel.

"I need to go." That's all he says, turning the handle and walking out of my office. He looks as if nothing just happened, except to me he's ruffled up.

Dallas is there just outside his office eyeing Clayton up and down, posturing to him his outward dislike. Clayton stops just shy of him, looking around the waiting room, little pups all on their mother's laps or shoulders. He inhales again before walking out the front door.

Kimberly steps out from behind me, tucking a stray piece of hair behind her ear. She's looking very uncomfortable.

"Next time, leave him home, or I'll pick you up from school, okay?" She just nods her head.

"Kimberly, listen. I want you coming to see me every week now. Just to make sure you're on the right track. If you don't start gaining weight, I'm going to start to eat all your meals with you, even at your school, so I suggest you start doing what you're told. I also will be speaking to your mother about this."

"I'll start eating more, I promise, but did you just see that?" Her excited voice hurts my ears.

"Yes." That's all I'm going to say about that.

"I need to text my mom." She pulls out her phone, and her fingers work at warp speed, sending the gossip out. I can't even stop her, she's so quick.

"I'll see you next week," I say, giving her a stern warning.

Finishing up after, I clean everything that needs cleaning. The clinic is empty now. They close early on Fridays.

Knocking on Aurora's office, I wait for her to answer. Dr. Valentine's door is still wide open.

"Come in, Rya."

"Aurora, I was just wondering—I know it's short notice—but I was wondering if you weren't doing anything tonight, would you like to go out for dinner with me?" I try to act casual, as it's the first time I have ever asked a friend out to dinner.

"I can't, babysitting the grandkids tonight." She's busy putting away files into the cabinet.

"Have fun. I was just thinking of grabbing something quick anyway. I have a lot of painting to do this weekend. See you Monday. Have fun tonight, Aurora."

"Have fun painting, Rya."

Walking away, I grab my purse from my office and shut the door behind me. I keep my head down as I get into my car. It's a quiet drive home, no music…I don't feel like listening to anything.

After the first coat of paint is applied to the walls in my bedroom, I stand back, looking at the color. I think agreeable grey is perfect. Ordering my dinner from the restaurant twenty minutes down the road, I clean the splatters of paint off my cheeks and arms, trying to make myself look halfway presentable.

The place is packed with people out having a fun Friday night. All the tables are full. As I make my way toward the bar for my pick up, I notice Dr. Valentine with a few pack members having drinks and eating wings. I'm not sure if he notices me or not; it doesn't seem that he does. He's giving the female beside him such a sinfully attractive smile that I have to swallow down the growl that wants to bubble up. The female's trying to feel his hair. Grabbing her hand, he shakes his head no at her. His buddies are talking to the other cute females at the table. I just have to tell myself it was just a kiss.

He looks up, catching me watching him. Turning away, I try to hide my embarrassment while waiting for my white Styrofoam container that's my dining partner tonight. At least I don't have to do dishes. Looking into the mirror behind the bar, I can see that Clayton is here with his sister. It's just the two of them, plates of food on the table. They're laughing together. He looks like he's teasing her, poking her shoulder with his finger. She tries to text something, and he grabs her phone away, putting it beside him. It's nice to watch them until he looks up and I have to look away.

Finally, the food's ready. Taking my single container, I walk out with as much dignity as a female on a Friday night alone can have.

After finishing the food and the rest of the painting, it's time for me to get comfortable.

An enchantment sets in, lighting the fire for the first time in my home. I can picture many nights snuggling by the fireplace, being lulled by the crackles and flickers of the flame. I bring my duvet out, laying it just a few feet away from the dancing light. Brushing my hair out from my shower, I let the heat dry it while sipping a glass of a red.

Dr. Valentine finds me sitting cross-legged on the floor, getting drunk in my underwear and shirt. He just opens the door like he belongs here with me. He stares at me on the floor.

"Let the pain begin." He says this to himself. Stepping closer, his eyes meet mine, with a sultry hunger no longer veiled. He's looking at me like he knows exactly what he wants and he's going to take it.

CHAPTER 11

First Steps

Exhale…

That's what I do when he closes the door behind him.

Inhale…

That's what I do when he takes that first step toward me.

"Why are you here?" His eyes reflect the orange flames from the fire.

He takes another step toward me. He looks like silence, quiet, calm…before the storm.

He takes another step without hesitance, and his shadow decides to fall over me. Can you feel shadows? At this moment, I think I can.

Heat from the fire is warm on the outside of my skin. Inside…I'm starting to blaze up.

"I had to come." The low timbre of his voice plays across my ears. It's sexy, making my heart start to double-dutch. He looks at me, eyes trailing down, starting with my face, working down to my chest…I'm not cold, but he'll notice the way I'm poking against the material of my shirt. They're achingly hard, needing touch. He's eliciting need.

He licks his teeth. This wolf excites me. My body slightly rocks back and forth, a small pressure deep inside starting to make its presence known. I can smell me, veins dilating, pheromones seeping out of open pores, calling out to the male how willing I am. No force needed on his part.

"You have no idea what you look like at this moment." He can barely get the words out; they sound deep with the thickness of a male whose throat is tightening with his own need.

He looks at my crossed legs until he focuses on the little silky material that covers up my female virtue. Is there a wet spot yet? Because right now, I feel as if there could be. He's looking at me as if I am some kind of masterpiece that needs to be revered. He pulls his gaze away, only to look back down once more between the opening of my legs. A rumble deep inside him shakes me slightly. Male wolves are so visual. He sniffs the air. A few more strides and he's directly in front of me.

He's of a marvelous design, no delusions to cloud my judgment.

Taking the wine glass out of my hand, he stretches himself away from me as he puts it down far away from us, as if he's afraid it might spill.

"I know where this will lead in the end. I know how this will turn out for me." He's looking at my eyes again, searching for something.

"Then why come?" My voice is low, barely above a whisper. His fingers are in my hair, pulling and twisting it in his grip. He pulls down slightly, and my lips are raised to him.

"Because there might be a chance that it doesn't go how I think it will. I have to take that chance, no matter how small I think it is." He pulls down more on my hair, angling my head so my whole throat is exposed to him. Starting on my jaw line, he traces it with his tongue. Nibbling at my earlobe, he pulls it into his mouth and sucks at it, teeth nipping slightly.

He sighs. Better still, a small little moan escapes his parted lips as he kisses down my neck. Teeth just barely graze my collarbone. His palm is just below the curve of my hips, thumb resting on the band of my underwear. Fingers grip the soft flesh, leaving an imprint that he is here. He smells of a sensual spice. I can feel his breath all over my skin.

He's on my mouth, kissing me at the same time he pushes me down into that crimson duvet. I'm on a cloud, and my sun is on top of me.

Tracing the outline of my lips with his tongue, he sucks in my bottom lip for just a second before he releases it. He's looking down at me, just staring.

I'm melting.

His hand starts to roam underneath my shirt while he gazes at me, watching me. I never knew how good fingers could feel against my ribcage. Can he feel me shudder underneath his touch?

My skin tingles with the path he's taking, legs weak and spread wide for him to rub himself against. If I didn't have a damp spot before, I do now. I'm saturating the material that barely covers me.

Moaning when he applies more pressure against

me, I wrap my legs around his calves. I meet his thrust through clothes. Deep pressure starts to make itself known to me, and I want to just stay like this, rubbing up against him while he touches my chest, kisses my lips.

The wolf in me surfaces slightly with a growl of approval. She likes this male wolf. She likes his advances. My muscles grow tighter with a need to shift, and claws swipe against his shirt, tearing the material easily. I smell his blood; I went a little too deep. That brings his face to mine, his wolf ascending slightly, looking at me. He sniffs against my cheek, a hot puff of breath as he stills on top of me. His hardness is between my legs. He doesn't pull away from my core.

Now his hand is on my thigh, slowly going up. I suck in a big breath. I have never had a male so close.

Dipping his head close to my ear, he asks, "Do you want me to stop?" I hesitate. Do I want him to stop?

"I don't know." It's best to stick with the truth.

He angles himself to the side of me, still pressed close, but not between my legs anymore.

"We need to stop until you can say 'don't stop.'" His finger traces my lips, my eyelids, my nose.

"Let's talk, okay?" Standing, he gets up from his spot, looks in my cupboards, and pulls out a glass. He pours himself some red. He picks up my wine glass from the floor and hands it to me as I sit upright once again.

The fire is casting soft light in the darkened room. His face glows from the flames.

He takes a drink from his glass, licking his lips after.

"I never expected this…you. I never expected to feel so much for a female again." He looks into the fire. Are memories playing on his mind?

"I feel guilty for this." He closes his eyes, a heart pain trying to bubble up.

"I understand." My shoulders hunch slightly forward.

"Rya, I want to be here with you. I think she would want this." His jaw clenches slightly, and he closes his eyes. A quiet descends as we both stare at the flames consuming the logs breaking and eating away at them until only ash will be left.

"I couldn't believe when I saw you that first day. I thought you were going to be a female who wasn't very pleasing to the eyes, that somehow was defective. How could a mate be rejected? It must be because they are not worthy. The way the pack talked about you, I was worried you really shouldn't be a midwife." His words make my stomach clench with what everyone must think of me.

Ugly, unworthy, defective.

"I even went to the Luna of this pack and stated my concerns. She just asked me to give you a chance, if I felt that you were unsafe in any way, she would pull you from your duties, but that you just needed a chance to prove yourself." He's still looking into the hypnotizing flames. He finishes his glass before I take a second sip. He places his glass close to the fireplace.

"When I came into the clinic that day, I knew instantly that everything I heard about you was lies.

How can someone blessed with the moon's eyes be anything but beautiful inside and out? So I watched you with those females, and I began to understand how truly special and overlooked you are." Sipping the red wine, I look at its color. It could pass for shades when falling in love or shades of rage…

"I'm still having a hard time trying to understand what happened to you. How could they all not see you?" This is some of the most hurtful, nicest truths I have ever heard.

"Clayton came to my house the night after I told you to lock your door. He was waiting for me. The look in his eyes was that of a male wanting to kill his competition. It was him and me, no witnesses. I was ready for him. I knew he'd come. I could smell his scent all over your house when I left." Dallas gets up, turning me so I'm facing the fire. He's behind me. His hands start to massage my shoulders over my shirt. It's relaxing the tension that I feel.

"He doesn't want you, Rya, but he doesn't want any other male to have you, either." This enrages me. He's ruined my past, and now he's tampering with my future.

"When he said that, I don't know what happened…I just attacked him. I wanted him to hurt the way you're hurting. So I went for his throat. He was shocked." Dallas rubs my lower back as he speaks, and it's calming me.

"You could get in a lot of trouble for that." My warning is from first-hand experience.

"What's he going to do, go tell his daddy that I hit him? He would look weak to his pack, that he couldn't settle his battles himself. The key is to have no witnesses. He came to my house alone at night looking to start a fight. It's not settled between us, but it will be soon." I can feel the smile on his face while he places a kiss on my shoulder.

"I'm not afraid of him, Rya. I want you to know this. I am not afraid of that male." He says it with conviction. He continues to rub my back, working all the muscles in his skilled hands. I've never experienced a back rub before by a male. It's a first for me.

Dallas lays me down so I'm facing the fire. He just keeps rubbing, massaging, and talking to me until I feel my eyes close with his sweet voice in my ear.

With the sun stirring the world awake, I gradually wake up. I'm shocked to be laying against Dallas's chest.

His arm is around my lower back.

I lay still for just a few minutes. His knee rests perfectly between my legs. When I rock with the slightest movement, a warm tingle starts to spread within me.

This feels good.

I rock again with the merest of movements, creating more pressure against my center. Stifling a moan, I press my chest against him. My breasts ache with the thought of his hands on them, his tongue, his teeth pulling at them.

Looking to see if he's awake, his eyes are still closed. I want to get up and move away, but I continue to rock against him subtly.

I can't believe I'm doing this, and I can't believe I can't stop myself.

This feels much better than a pillow.

He still hasn't opened his eyes, so I continue my forward and backward motion against him. A little whimper comes out of my mouth. It's then that I feel his hands travel to my hips to pull me up against his maleness.

His turn to release a quiet sleepy moan, hands roaming all over my flesh.

The fire's out, but right now I'm ablaze. He's feeling every line the whip made but not saying a word.

I pull myself into a sitting position, hair falling over my shoulders. He begins to feel me where no male has never been before.

My body floods itself with thanks to this male's touch.

He smells delicious.

A howl wants to break out, as I start to really get close to what no male has ever given me before.

Exquisite.

This feels so good.

"You're beautiful." He's staring.

That just set me on the edge...teetering that one second before all of my body's pleasure consumes me. He approves with the way his canines are out, looking at my neck.

That sight sends another wave through me, that I can even affect a male this way. He's making me feel *beautiful*, *wanted*.

I lay against his chest, and he strokes my hair, kissing my head. I don't want to get up. He's warm, and he fits my body well.

My hand on his hip travels downward. I'm

nervous. I have never felt a male this way.

Dallas grabs my hand, kissing the fingertips. "You don't have to do that."

"I want to." He closes his eyes, releasing my hand.

I move my hand down his chest, to his hip. Down the side of his groin and upper thigh. Letting my finger feel his skin. I can smell his pleasure from this. I can feel those fine muscles twitching under my touch. He lets out a breath when I bend down, placing a kiss along the side of his ribs, down to where the band of his boxers meets skin.

I look at him, and our eyes connect. He takes a small breath as skin touches skin. His lips part as he exhales out, closing them for a brief second. He moans his appreciation at having hands touch him. Dallas's muscles in his abdomen give me a show as he starts to find his own personal rhythm.

He's trembling in pleasure.

The moan that he gives vibrates my thighs. This is a full-grown male rumble of ecstasy.

He's losing his control. His fingers are clenching the duvet. His eyes open, and that hand goes into my hair, bringing me against his lips. Kissing me hard, his teeth cut into my lips. He lets his growl shake us, his smell now potent. It's a powerful smell that draws the wolf in me out. She's been so dormant for so long that she's near the surface...a ripple of skin, a flash of teeth his way. It's somewhat painful as my jaw starts to stretch on its own. She wants to meet him, the only male who has shown us beauty.

His hand on my hair takes the strays away from

my wolf's eyes.

"Shift for me, Rya." He's got a commanding voice that I haven't heard from him before.

I fight the wolf on this. I haven't shifted in many years. I don't want him to witness this.

"No, I can't." It's painful fighting your own nature inside yourself.

So he sits and waits for the winner to emerge. Once I get control of myself again, I feel embarrassed.

"I'm sorry, she has never done that to me."

"How long have you gone without a shift?" He's getting up going to the bathroom, letting the tap water run.

"It's been six years." He walks out of the bathroom. He's cleaned himself off.

"That's not healthy. You need to shift. Maybe, later on, we could introduce our furs to each other. Maybe on Sunday after my family leaves."

"Your family's coming for a visit?"

"My mother has had this visit scheduled for the longest time. She and my brothers will all be here. I expect you for dinner at my house tonight." He doesn't leave room for any argument.

"I'm not sure." My head goes down again. They won't like me.

"My family won't bite, I promise." He gives me a sly smile, making his eyes crinkle at the sides. "Don't be afraid of them. They'll like you." He's standing up now in front of me. I wrap the duvet around my body. I feel exposed now that the heat between us has cooled down.

"How many brothers do you have?"

"I have four. I'm the oldest." He looks at me as if I should say something. When I don't, he smiles to himself.

"Go get dressed. I'll take you out for breakfast." He's already putting his clothes on from last night. Unfortunately, I have ruined his shirt. He'll need to go home and change first.

"I should shower first." My body reeks with lust.

"No! I want everyone to smell us," he says, a feral look in his eyes.

"We won't hide this from the wolves. I want them all to know what I am doing with you." That makes me smile. He doesn't want to hide me in the closet. He wants everyone to understand I have someone who is interested in me…that I have a male and he's *it*.

CHAPTER 12

Trash/Treasure

Waffles and milkshakes start our day.
This isn't your greasy breakfast joint. It's hipster chic…waiters with wiry beards and soft brown hues serve us. Wearing their beanies, tattoos that travel the length of their arms, plugs in ears. Pants that sag slightly in the ass. The background music is indie, playing songs I have never heard of, but the hipsters, they are all humming along to the tunes.

My fork crunches through the top crust of the golden waffle, digging into the soft fleshy middle. I ordered a vanilla fried waffle, with cinnamon and maple-poached apples, topped with coffee whipped cream. I close my eyes slightly with every bite.

The coconut vanilla chai milkshake is so thick I feel like I should use a spoon to eat it instead of trying to suck it through the straw. My cheeks pull in with the effort. Dallas is wide-eyed watching me, a flush creeping on his face, his hands going underneath the table.

121

"Rya, can I ask you a question?"

"Sure." I sip my shake again.

"Have you dated many wolves or humans?" I choke on the thick liquid in my mouth.

"No, Dallas, this is actually my first date. Does this count as a date?"

He smiles at me. "You haven't been on a date before?"

"No." I shake my head, not meeting his eyes.

"Really?" He's surprised.

"Dallas, you were the first male that I have ever kissed." My confession makes me turn that shade of red I was drinking last night. He stills in his seat, big breath in, and a big breath out.

Kimberly and a few other juvenile females I don't know sit down just a few tables away. I smile toward them; they are the only other wolves in this human place. Out of the corner of my eye, I notice their heads tilted up, scenting the air. They all look at each other, leaning in, soft whispers. Phones come out, fast fingers spreading the news like wildfire through a forest deep in a drought. They remind me so much of my youth, the cool girls…the untouchables…the ones who could make your high school years miserable or bearable. They have no power over me anymore. I'm a full-grown female, not an impressionable juvenile that just wanted to fit in.

Kimberly holds my eyes, a judgment behind them, as if I am in the wrong, as if they just caught me cheating on my mate. She must feel all puffed up by her friends, who surround her with confidence. I hold those eyes of hers until her confidence fails her, and she looks away with her tail curled under.

Dallas takes my milkshake away, sucking it back using the same straw I just had my lips on. He smiles with his teeth, showcasing them to the females. They get all big eyed, shoulders hunching forward. It's not a threat; it's just meant to say, "I see what you're doing, and I don't like it."

Curiously enough, some more pack members start to arrive, gawking at the sight in front of them until more wolves than humans populate the place.

The alpha saunters in with his two betas in tow...big males with scowls on their faces. I see Dallas prickle up slightly. Tense muscles twitch in his jaw, and he leans back in the booth, legs spread wide, with a wickedly sexy smile on his face.

The males approach our tables, mouths open with the breaths they are taking. Quiet settles in, the hushed voices only creating a deeper quiet...like it's waiting for something to break it.

The three are standing shoulder to shoulder, almost touching. One is Kennedy's father, the Alpha's best friend, raised together like brothers. Dallas looks up to all three of them, meeting each of their eyes. I'm holding my breath, waiting for that silence to break.

The Alpha's fingers tap on the table before he leans in close to Dallas's ear. "Do you understand what you're doing?"

"Perfectly." It's Dallas's turn to lean into the Alpha.

"Rya." His focus is on me now.

"Why don't we set up a meeting? I think we

should have a sit-down and discuss some things that are important to the pack's future." His head is turned to the rest of the wolves in the room. It's as if I have already decided I would meet with him.

"You're right. I do need to discuss some stuff with you. I applied for a transfer out of this pack, but the Luna won't allow it. I expect that you can have a talk with her, let her know that it's my choice that I choose to leave. She might not like my choice, but it's mine to make." His hands are off the table now.

"We don't have a replacement for you." He just walks away from me. The conversation is shut down. Taking a seat close to the door, they order breakfast while the wolves look on.

"You want a transfer out?"

"I did." He smiles.

"You did?" His eyebrows shoot up in question. Cutting into his waffle, he takes a bite, leaving a little on the fork before putting it up to my lips to finish the rest.

"I have two years left on this contract. After that, I get to go wherever I want. Maybe I could go home." He's looking as if big decisions are resting on his shoulders. "Maybe you could come with me if things work out?" I take the bite from his fork, the food he's offering me in front of the watching eyes of pack members. I hear some rumbling growls from the wolves eating breakfast around us. Not very loud, it's on the lower level of the hearing spectrum, but loud enough for them to sound their displeasure.

It would be a great loss to any pack to lose their

midwife but a disaster to lose a doctor. How long have they been searching, recruiting, to find him? Dr. Peters must have been in his early eighties when Dallas came. So I'm not sure if their rumbling is about me going with Dallas or about him stating that he might leave.

"Ready to go." Dallas puts money on the table, paying my share of the bill.

With one more long pull on the milkshake, I take Dallas's hand. We walk out, Dallas leading the way until we get to the door. He opens it for me, allowing me to brush by him. He follows behind, taking all their stares against his back while protecting mine.

Getting into the car, he kisses my lips. He tastes like my milkshake, vanilla with chai…yum.

The ride to my home is perfect. His hand is on my thigh. Can he smell me again? I'm dying for a repeat of last night.

"Please come tonight. I really want my family to meet you." He's kissing my wrist as we sit in my driveway.

"I'll come over. What time again?" I'm breathless, his tongue licking at my pulse.

"Five, come over at five." His lips are on the side of my neck, sucking in the skin. Teeth are grazing the spot that holds marks of mates. I'm not sure I can get out of the car, my skin is so warm. He's kissing me like in the movies…

His phone starts to ring. With a sigh, he pulls away.

"Hello." He's annoyed. His voice lets the other person on the line understand this.

"Luna Catherine, so good to hear from you." He gives me a wink.

"I can't meet with you today. My mother should be at my house very soon. Unless...why don't you come over tonight after dinner?" He's rolling his eyes while listening to her talk.

"That sounds good. See you around six-thirty." He hangs up his phone, laughing.

"Seems that the Luna is very interested in my personal life all of a sudden."

I try to talk, but he's kissing me again.

"I don't want you to worry about anything, Rya. My mom will absolutely love to talk to this Luna about my personal life. You should go before I just follow you inside and do lots of new things to you." I shiver in my own skin with the thought.

***

Walking up the path to his home, I balance a pumpkin pie in hand. I slow roasted the pumpkin all afternoon in cinnamon, vanilla, and brown sugar. Golden flakes of butter crust hold the contents in place. I brought a little bowl with cold whipped cream to put on top if they like. I couldn't come empty handed. That would be rude.

Breathe.

My stomach is doing some flip-flopping lurches as I knock on the door. *Please let them like me.* Smelling the pie, I let it coat my brain, softening my nerves. I see the family at the table. That's different from when I was here last. They are laughing, smiling. It looks like a picture should be taken.

Dallas opens the door. He looks nervous as well.

"Come in, Rya." Entering, everyone's eyes turn to mine. Four big males stare into my eyes, not looking away, open mouthed. His mother gets up from her spot. She sniffs the air. Thank the moon I scrubbed myself clean. It would be mortifying meeting her for the first time with his scent all over me.

Surrounded by soft strands of medium caramel hair, her eyes look like miniature small earths from far away. She's of medium build but carries herself with dignity. Shoulders back, spine straight, she approaches. It takes all my resolve to stand up straight and greet her at her level. I don't slouch; I don't look away.

"Rya, this is my mother." He gives a slight pause before saying her name. "Grace. Mom, this is Rya." She gives him a look but says nothing to her son.

"Rya, it's nice to meet you." She presses her cheek against mine, inhaling my neck. I can almost feel her lips press against my skin.

"It's nice to meet you as well, Grace." A soft, comforting smile touches her eyes.

"Rya, these are my brothers." With his hand, he points to *Caleb*, *Cash*, *Carson*, *Crane*…

They all bow slightly to me, but not touching me. Males don't touch other males' interests, even brothers.

His mother takes the pie out of my hand, putting it on the table…but not before smelling it.

"Did you make this yourself?" she questions.

"Yes, I had some pumpkin in the garden, so I thought I should use it up instead of it going to waste." I'm so nervous I can hardly think. They're all looking at me. *Please like me.*

"That's so smart of you. I hate when things go to waste." She's giving me a once-over.

"Come sit down with us." I'm not sure where my place is. I know where my place at my parents' house is, I know where I belong at my own house, but I have never been invited to sit at anyone else's table beside my teacher, and that was just the two of us.

His mother makes it easy for me as she pulls out a seat to Dallas's right. He's at the head; I take the right, and Caleb—I think that's his name—takes the left. His mother sits at the other end of the table. Food, lots of food, is piled high on serving plates. Lots of slow-roasted buttery vegetables of every kind. There's a roast that looks like you could cut it with the edge of your fork. Biscuits and rich, thick gravy. Sweet tea in pitchers filled with ice.

Dallas puts his hand over mine, giving it a squeeze. Can he tell how nervous I am? His brothers are giving me the side-eye.

"Rya, I'm told that you're the midwife here."

"Yes, I am." I just can't put the food in my mouth. My nerves are making me slightly sick.

"Your parents must be very proud of you." She's smiling, not really eating her meal, just drinking that sweet tea.

"They are." I tell the truth because they are proud of what I have accomplished.

I sip my glass of tea. It's a rich brown in the heavy crystal glass. Ice cubes clink together in the swirl of liquid.

"Rya, I know all about you—" My throat tightens.

"I should go." I say it to Dallas as I take a step away from the table. I just can't have her judging me. She must know my own mate rejected me, that somehow she must know I'm defective in some way for her son.

"Mother," he roars, and I shake. A knock on the door swings everyone's eyes to the intruder.

The door opens. Luna Catherine is here early with a smile on her face.

"Dallas, sorry I'm early, but I just wanted to drop by and say hello to your family." She's looking around the table. A slight bow to Grace. She's looking at the places everyone is sitting. Her eyes fall to mine and hold. Her jaw clenches slightly.

"Come in." He closes the door behind her.

Grace stands from her spot to greet the Luna.

"Luna Catherine, finally. It's nice to meet you."

"Luna Grace, so nice to put a face to the name." Both embrace quickly, no lingering touching.

My mouth is open as I look to Dallas, who's looking away from me. I try to catch his eye to try and ask why he didn't tell me his parents are pack leaders. I'm upset that he's kept something like this from me.

Luna Catherine eyes me, looking at my neck. She lets out a breath of relief.

"I like your new table, Dallas." Grace cringes slightly when she hears her son's name.

"Thank you. My mother just brought it for me today. A gift."

"Where did you find such a masterpiece?" I think that Luna Catherine is trying to start off light, compliment something before starting with the real stuff.

I look at the table more. It's dark oak that's been keenly carved with an artisan's care.

"I found this table at the side of the road. Could you imagine my reaction when I realized someone just threw this away?" She shakes her head with a click of her jaw. Her hand starts to trail along the edge of the table. A finger traces a stain that's buried deep in the wood.

"Sometimes people don't realize what they have in front of them until they see it again. It makes them realize what they actually did and regret throwing it away in the first place," Luna Catherine interjects.

"Very true. But once you throw something away, it's up for grabs to anyone who wants to put the time in to make it beautiful again." Luna Grace is staring now into the other Luna's eyes.

"This will be a very good addition to my son's future. It's strong, solid, has a good base. There might be little stains here and there, a nick in some spots, but I think it gives it character. What do you think?" A very smug look comes across his mother's face.

"Yes, very true, but I think the owner of the table could come back. Maybe make an offer that benefits both parties?" Just like politicians, these Lunas speak their own language.

"No, this table is very special...blue moon special. No offer would be good enough. How does that saying go…" She taps her chin. "One wolf's trash is another's treasure."

Luna Catherine postures herself to Luna Grace, showing molten black eyes. It's as if she has a scorpion's tail curled, ready to strike. All four brothers get up from their seats at the same time. Heavy growls rumble out of their chests. They don't like what they're witnessing.

"I think, Luna Catherine, it's time for you to leave. Everyone's fur is getting a little ruffled." Dallas opens the door.

"Rya, we will talk very soon." She turns those dark eyes to me before walking out. I'm screwed.

She closes the door behind her, and the whole group takes a calming breath.

"I think you could take her, Mom." Is it Caleb that says this or Crane?

"Rya, I didn't mean to offend you by saying I know about you. I only meant that I know about the hardship you have faced." She brings me into a hug, smoothing my hair down.

I turn my head to Dallas as I am in his mother's embrace. "Why didn't you tell me you're an Alpha?"

His mother pulls away from me. "Because he isn't an Alpha, his father is. After his mate died…" The grief in the Luna's eyes makes my eyes want to water.

"After his mate died, he decided to become a doctor, someone different, instead of following his true path. I think it took his mind off her death because he was so consumed with studying that he couldn't think too much." His brothers look uncomfortable with all this emotion coming from their mother.

"We're preparing for when the time comes for my mate to step down as Alpha and how the challenges will work without destroying our pack. Unless my son changes his mind and decides to claim what's his." Hopeful eyes all turn toward Dallas.

"There's a lot to think about. I'm not ready yet to make a decision on that." He's looking at me when he says this, like I'm the answer he's looking for.

She brings me back to my place beside her son at the head of the table. We spend the rest of the night talking about his childhood, his pack, how big it is—easily it's triple the size of my pack. We also talk about his mate and how wonderful she was. It doesn't get me jealous. I just feel so bad that he lost someone so precious. He tells me the story of when he found her the first time, he claimed her immediately. They were together one year before she died in a boating accident.

I look at his neck. The claimed mark has faded away, as if his mate never existed. It must be sad for the living to slowly watch the mark fade away...nothing they can do about it but watch. It allows them to be claimed by someone else when enough time has passed.

"I should be going." Standing, I say goodbye to the brothers, who all bow slightly in respect. The Luna embraces me again.

"Anytime you want into our pack, all you have to do is show up and we will take you in." She really means what she's saying.

"I would start a war," I say sadly.

"Wars have been fought for much less. If my son wants this, the whole pack will stand behind him." Her teeth flash her white of war.

"I'll walk you out." His hand is on my back, very close to the curve of my ass.

When we reach my car, we pause. I lean against it, facing him. "Thank you for coming and meeting my family. Next is my father, but we have to go to my pack for that." His head dips low, and he kisses me.

"Why didn't you tell me you're a future Alpha?" I still feel slightly betrayed that he held this information from me.

"I didn't think it was important until now. I don't like to advertise this too much, especially when I had no intention of taking my birthright. Forgive me. I won't keep anything like this from you again, okay?"

I nod my head. "Okay," I say quietly.

He closes the door with a small wave.

It's not a very long drive back. I get out of the car, and my nose curls up with the smell of a wolf claiming territory. The smell is ammonia strong, pungent, making my eyes water. Quickly looking around, I search for him among the trees.

My door has long scratch marks gouged into the wood. I see a tree to the side of me down. Another one is toppled onto my garden, which lays barren now.

"I just want to talk to you." His voice scares me, prickling down my spine. He's holding himself against a tree, claws dug in as anchors.

133

"Let me just talk to you, Rya." He growls out my name, jaw clenching. His body looks like it's dueling with itself. Snarling fangs poke out of gums. A tendon snaps bone, only to realign again.

"I don't want to talk. You've said more than enough to last me a lifetime." I try to get my keys out. My hands are shaking. One clawed hand unhooks itself from the tree, deep heavy growls vibrating into me. My wolf rises up inside me. Blood…she wants the blood from his throat.

I scream slightly with the pain of nails that push from my skin. His other hand just swipes away the thick chunk of wood like it's nothing, and the tree topples with a groan and creak.

His step is awkward as a hip tries to shift into his fighting form. Scalpel blades feel like they are pushing themselves through my nail beds. I'm sweating from the pain, and I almost retch my dinner up beside my door.

He's so close now his breath hits my face. My body pulses with a life of its own…an arch of electricity from him to me joins us. His nose goes into my neck, inhaling. His teeth have descended. His fist hits my door, shaking the foundation of the building. I can't breathe.

He gives me a full-grown male wolf growl, ringing my ears deaf from the noise. With another inhale of my scent, he presses himself against me. His hand takes my extended claws in his, easily pinning my arms above my head. His eyes are no longer green but that of a wolf who is going to do what he has always wanted to do.

His other hand turns my neck to the side, while

his chest presses into me. A tongue slides out, tasting a mate's flesh for the first time. He groans, shaking his whole body. I try to break his hold, but it's impossible. I can't even kick hard enough to have him feel it. They will leave bruises, but right now he doesn't notice it.

"Clayton, what are you doing?" Kennedy's voice, full of pain, hits his back like darts.

I look at her. It's as if a wife just caught her husband cheating on her. She looks the way I looked when he chose her over me.

CHAPTER 13

Love Mark

Mother Earth hears her cries. Her tears start to wet the dirt. The moon is shining down on them, her light giving a spotlight show.

"Why?" Her voice sounds fragile. Her heart must be causing her pain because she's clutching at her chest. Isn't love supposed to bring you pleasure?

His wolf is still half out, smelling my neck as his skin side tries to pull his head away. The wolf snaps its jaws toward Kennedy; the loud click of teeth can't be missed. He does this again, snapping its jaw. Violent waves spasm his skin from the inside, ripping the flesh. He's back at my neck, smelling, licking flesh. A heartbreaking whimper pours out his throat. His forehead touches mine. The wolf's eyes meet mine and hold. His nose is touching, nudging into me. Another raw whimper hits my ears.

The wolf does not look away. The both of us are very still now. His half-clawed hand brushes against my cheek, sniffing inside my mouth. A tear—a stray, lonely tear—starts its descent downward. Its path is blocked by whiskers trying to poke through clean flesh. Another whimper from the fur side calls to my soul, as if he's in agony.

The wolf starts to cry its song out for the moon to hear, a begging, a pleading.

His nature is only wanting to breathe in. Writhing, twisting on himself, he uses my body to hold himself up as bones break, muscles tear, only to try to go back again. Groans tumble out his mouth, along with great, high-pitched whines. His lips pull back in a snarl to Kennedy, snapping at her while nuzzling me, gently biting my jaw without leaving marks.

Panting in, breathing out.

I'm watching a war unfold where both sides are even matches. Which constitution will win?

The turning point in the battle comes when his dense green eyes turn toward Kennedy, and his nails retract. He calms as residual spasms shudder out. He's still resting against me, no space between us. He's like a rock, hardened without give.

I inhale him in, nose touching skin.

Now he turns to me, his eyes on mine. Our noses are so close, the tips almost touch. His hand comes up exactly like his wolf just did, except no claws are out. Just his flesh touching my flesh.

Magnetic, the draw to him is intense. Raw moon power pulls us toward each other in a collision of epic proportion.

"Clayton." It's choked out, a desperate wail. Her hands are now gripping into the earth as if it could somehow provide her with support. Her heart is shredding. She looks like a perfect broken picture, shattered, destroyed beyond repair.

He takes a step away from me, going to her. He kneels with her now. His knees will stain with grass.

"Why?" The both of them face each other.

"I can't explain it," he says with a shake of his head.

"Do you love her?" Her lips tremble, little hiccups coming out every now and then. Her tears don't stop.

"No, I love you."

"Then why are you here?" Her voice is so soft while she looks into his eyes.

"I can't help myself. I can't fight it anymore." She starts to sob. He holds her to his chest, her head resting on his shoulder.

He's her rock. Too bad it's starting to crack and crumble apart right underneath her.

"What's going to happen?" she asks him, like he has answers.

"I don't know." His lips are on her forehead. Not the answer she was looking for as she starts retching on my lawn. Bile from the pit of her stomach is making its way out.

I'm standing there watching them. Is this how marriages fall apart, with one party being attracted to another, not in love but in lust? Willing to break trust for just a taste of that wicked desire?

"I don't want him. He has nothing I need," I say to the both of them. I watch as his shoulders tense up, while she holds him closer to her.

"I need you," he says to me. He looks at Kennedy. "But I love you."

"You can't have me!" My voice raises to a harsh hiss.

"I'll fight for you. You're worth my fight. I could kill her, sever the bond. You would be only mine." She has his head in her hands as she tells him this. He looks at me, contemplating her offer.

Part of me wants to give Kennedy and Clayton western justice. I look toward a tree, trying to find a branch that can support both their weights. They went into this together; they can go out together. Death is absolute, and I have fantasized, if given the opportunity again, could I end her? Could I drink from the throat of life? I can't. He's just not worth that need in me anymore.

I don't need to see that fantasy fulfilled.

His wolf strikes her throat hard, clamping it in his powerful jaw. He's on all fours now, skin changing to fur. Blood starts to pool underneath Kennedy as her fists start hitting a back that is curving, stretching his shirt so tight it's splitting down the middle. His wolf has decided he's thirsty and needs to drink from her throat of life. He must not have taken too kindly to her threat. The wolf has just taken a giant leap into insanity.

His head shakes back and forth, tearing at the skin, ripping it apart as if it were the haunches of a deer. Her body swings back and forth with the force, hands hanging limply at her side. Blood, more blood than I have ever seen, is oozing out from her gaping wounds. She doesn't look like herself, eyes half open, lips parted and blue tinged.

He gets control of himself. With shaky hands, he tries to stop the bleeding.

"What have you done?" Running toward them, I see he's trying to stop the flow of blood with his fingers, but it's seeping out the cracks. Now instead of grass stains, he wears his moon's blood while the real one watches on.

"Put her in my car." Racing, I open the back door. Her breath is bubbling, gurgling out.

I'm shaking, barely able to concentrate on the road and dialing his number.

"Dallas, you need to come to the clinic. It's an emergency." I can't hide the urgency that borderlines hysteria in my voice.

He has her in his hands, rocking back and forth. "What have I done? Don't die. Stay with me, Kennedy." She's unresponsive.

Getting her on the operating room table, I try to get out what I think he might need, trying to recall all my emergency training that I have never had to use before. They only train you for the what ifs. I've never had a what if until *now*.

Opening bandages, I put tight pressure on her neck to stop the flow of blood. I have to be careful not to put too much pressure or else she can't breathe. She's only taking little shallow breaths. They gurgle in her throat. It's as if she's drowning in her own blood.

Dallas walks in, calm, getting stuff from the shelves. His hands don't shake like mine are. Uncovering the bandage, he looks at it, pulling apart the flesh, seeing how deep down it goes. Putting the bandage back on, he presses my hands more firmly on her throat.

"Did you do this?" He's asking a question that he really doesn't want the answer to. He's getting out steel trays wrapped in blue cloth, opening them up to reveal silver-tipped instruments that are able to cut through our skin easily...but they leave scars.

"No, I did." Clayton's ready for the fallout.

"You need to call her parents. They need to be here. She might not make it. Now get out, and don't come back in."

"I'm not leaving her." He makes a stand. One by one, Dallas's brothers make it into the small room, crowding the space. Dallas just concentrates on what's before him.

"You need to help me, Rya. Can you do this?" I nod my head yes, still applying pressure. Her skin is purplish, red, as the blood withdraws from her extremities to try and save her vital organs. Her nail beds are bluish, and she's cool to the touch. A deep breath in, then a pause...I wait until another breath is taken in at irregular intervals. Her lungs seem like they have the death rattle.

I watch as his steady hands put an intravenous into her arm, connecting it to a line that's attached to a bag of blood. He turns it on wide open as the life pours into her.

"I won't leave!" Clayton screams out to all of them. All Dallas does is look at the second oldest. It's just a look before all four brothers are on him instantly. Unlike me, he feels every punch that comes his way, bone-crunching pain as the brothers do what the good doctor wants. He puts up a fight, crushing bones with his fists, which the brothers return in kind.

"Call her parents," Dallas says once more to him. I'm not sure he heard. The door closes behind them, leaving us alone with the dying female.

"Okay, Rya, see this bag of blood? I never want the line to run dry. Keep an eye on it. The blood's in the fridge. Take out another ten bags from the freezer. They need to be put in that warmer over there to thaw them out." I do what he tells me to.

He's pulling the bandage away from her throat, injecting something into the wounds to make the bleeding slow down slightly. I don't see that an artery was hit. If it was, she would have bled out on my lawn.

She looks so peaceful now like she's just resting, ghost-like. He's suturing up her neck. Starting very deep, he pulls the skin together while working up, layer after layer. His gloved hands are all bloody.

"Can you suction her, Rya?" Turning on the suction machine, I stick the long hose down her throat. I put my thumb over the hole in the tubing, allowing the suction to remove blood in her lungs. Lots of blood is coming into the canister, filling it up crimson red.

I look at the bag; it's almost done. I reach into the fridge and change it out for the almost empty one, spiking the new bag of blood and hanging it on the pole again. Her color is starting to come around very slowly. He's injecting some more solution into her open flesh.

"What is that?" I stare at the syringe.

"It helps to constrict the blood vessels so the bleeding is more controlled." All his attention is on her. She's lucky; he just saved her life.

More bags of blood are emptied into her vein. After at least an hour of sewing her up, he's finished. As he washes his hands at the sink, I can't help but look at that ruined neck. She gets to wear the scars of their love for every wolf to see. These are not claimed scars; no, these are the scars of a wolf wanting to end a life.

Dallas picks her up, holding her close to his body, a bag of blood resting on her stomach.

I open the door for him to go into one of the recovery rooms. Aurora is waiting there, bed prepared, a pungent tea already brewing. Dallas places her on the bed while giving Aurora detailed instructions about what to do for the next few hours.

I hear soft crying from a female in the waiting room. Kennedy's mother is weeping into her mate's arms. Both stand up as Dallas approaches them.

"She's out of danger, but we need to give her more blood. You can see her now." Only her mother takes a step to the room; her father turns and walks out the door. Heavy rage seeps out of his body. Dallas cleans off the table, preparing another line of blood, as if expecting another patient to come through those doors very soon.

CHAPTER 14

Alpha Born

I watch Dallas as he tries to speak, but nothing comes out. His power is projecting into me. He's no longer the wolf I thought I knew. This is something that scares me, *frightens me.*

"His wolf attacked her, protecting me from the both of them." Teeth, sharp male canine teeth, descend slightly. His fighting form is trying to take the skin side over. Touching his head, I try to calm him, to settle his rising fur.

He turns from me, taking one step toward the door, then another step as fabric starts to stretch over muscles that are engorging with blood.

His brothers are watching the scene with guarded eyes, in silent stillness, their mother in the middle of them flanked on all sides.

Protecting their most precious.

They all look at him, nose in the air, sniffing testosterone that he's releasing. His body prepares for battle.

"Think this through." It's his mother who's in his ear instantly. She's calm, eyes watching everything.

"Think, watch, understand." Her words are her wisdom.

Outside, I look at the circle that's forming around Clayton. He's all puffed out. His face is red in rage, his veins dilating. I can see them on his forearms pulsing with his life. His shirt is torn, his moon's blood all over it, staining the fabric. His clothes will have to be thrown out. There's no saving them; they're ruined completely.

Kennedy's father points his finger in his face, but Clayton slaps it away.

"You people disgust me," Clayton spits out. "What do you think would happen? What do you think would be the outcome?" Clayton holds his ground not stepping back, while her father takes a step forward.

"We never expected this," Kennedy's father rages. A hard punch to Clayton's jaw does not stagger him. He takes it willingly, spitting out a mouthful of blood; maybe a tooth comes with it.

"You never expected this? You had us sleeping together since we were babies. When we were thirteen, you all knew what we were doing in that bed, but you all said nothing. You all encouraged it. We had your approval." Clayton's voice sounds slightly pained and tight. A purple, angry-looking bruise is blossoming open on his jaw line.

More wolves are showing up. They remind me of locusts devouring the sight in front of them.

"You all thought we would end up mates, and

when that didn't happen, you just wanted us to stop. How could you just stop loving someone? You can't!" he screams. Fists clenching, blood drips down onto the earth to soak up.

"We tried to break up, but we just couldn't. How can you when what we have is real?" His voice cracks.

"You were so happy that she attacked me, weren't you? Gave you the excuse to have her shunned by the pack, hoping I would change my mind, come around. Kept her nice and safe from any other wolf who might want to sniff her out." He's accusing his father now, pointing fingers in faces that need to be punched.

More wolves are showing up. I can see them eating up all this family business that should be kept behind closed doors. Except he's decided to air it all out on the line.

Clayton turns to Dallas, sizing him up and down. He gives a puff of exhaled breath as if he's absolutely no real threat to him.

"You're going to have to take a number." That's all he says to Dallas before turning slightly from him.

"We never thought this would happen," Luna Catherine interjects, her female voice sounding high in contrast to the males' lower threatening rumbles.

"What? Are you kidding me! You're the one who told her from birth that she was mine, what a beautiful daughter she is. You were grooming her from birth to be the next Luna. Do you know how bad Kennedy felt when you found out we weren't mates and you would take her away on 'hunting trips?'" His fingers make big quotations in the air.

"She loves you. You paraded her around. She never said anything to you because she just wanted you to like her again. She did everything you asked without complaint. She has done nothing wrong but love me." His voice cracks slightly. He's putting it all on the table for these wolves to feast on.

"I remember the day we sat both families down and told you we weren't mates. All of you crying, the tears you all shed for us. Then you said we had to stop!" He's toe to toe with his father now. Same size, one male on the edge of his prime, the other males on the edge of retirement.

"You thought what a strong bloodline we would make, what pups we would have. I remember the shock on your face, Mom, when you found out Rya was mine. The disappointment, a low rank going to take your spot. You couldn't believe it." Such skeletons he's revealing for all these wolves to see. Family business that should not be made public. He's showing their opinion of low ranks. Murmuring from the audience starts to grumble in outrage.

My head lowers at his words. I never really felt we were of low status. My father was a hard worker, and my mother made sure we were clean, fed, went to school. We never went without...ever. We had a good family until I met my *mate*.

"Look at her now, Mom! You must have been so surprised when she came back. Not the same little juvenile that left. No, not the same at all." He's looking at me now, up and down, his eyes loving what he's seeing.

147

"I hope you never get your claws into her. She's too good for this family." His mother looks like the inside of a great grandfather clock, gears shifting, turning, switching with her thoughts.

"I'm sorry, Rya. I would never end you. I don't have it in me. I feel so sorry you have someone like me as your mate. I have failed you, my pack, the moon. I just couldn't let her go." He's squaring up to both the Alpha and the Beta.

"I understand what's going to happen, and I welcome it." His words are spit in his father's face.

"You attacked my daughter!" The big beta's body blocks out Clayton's face.

"She threatened Rya. My wolf wanted the threat gone." All these males' eyes turn toward me. I hold them all with mine, not saying a word. What can be said?

"You know the punishment for attacking another pack member." The Alpha looks smaller to me now, not as big as he used to be.

"I do." He's resigned to his fate.

The winds starts to pick up. A maroon shadow from the moon falls across Clayton's face. Turning green eyes my way, he just holds me in my place. It's as if he's looking at me like it will be the last time he will ever see me again.

"I'm sorry." The apology is real, full of deep pain. I say nothing back. He doesn't look like he expected a response.

"Treat Rya like she deserves. Be good to her." Hard eyes bored into Dallas.

Stepping up to the third oldest brother, Cash, his jaw is clenching so tight I can hear teeth break. "As soon as she's well enough, claim her. Take her away from here." Cash snaps his teeth at Clayton being held back from his brother's big hands.

"She's the most beautiful female you will ever meet, and her heart is good. Just please give her a chance. She deserves to be truly happy." A clawed hand tries to swipe at Clayton's neck. He would be no match for him. Clayton would eat him.

"Stop." His mother breathes into his ear, a forceful command no higher than a whisper, and it stills him.

He gives another look to me before he walks toward his end.

The supple, worn leather handle rests easily in his hands. Generations of use have made the brown turn dark, shiny. The silver threading that has been woven into the braid is hundreds of years old, yet it does not fray at the end. The master weaver knew how to construct this to last generations. I wonder if our generation could ever make anything like this again.

The cold is starting to slither from behind, up my back like a snake, slowly creeping higher and higher, wrapping around my neck. I'm not sure I can bear witness to this sight, yet I'm paralyzed, unable to look away.

He's standing at the same pole where everyone stands. This pole doesn't recognize status, only pain. Everyone is equal while taking the whip's mark.

His hands are being bound, but not in the flimsy string that would tie a juvenile down. His are locked into place with big metal chains that fasten tight against skin, infused with a high concentration of silver. A full-grown male wolf should know how to behave by now. This is meant to hurt as much as possible.

His forehead rests against the pole, eyes closing. A tear already comes, not from the physical pain that he's about to endure, but the way his heart must be blowing apart inside himself.

He tilts his head up, and the moon greets his eyes. She sees everything in the night. Dark, dangerous when she has to be, beautiful, loving when her children need her to be. His father approaches him, a hand on his head while speaking soft words into his ear. His shirt is ripped off, his back exposing not pristine flesh untouched, but marked with silver-tipped needles.

KENNEDY is etched across his upper back, shoulder to shoulder. Big black ink dug deep into the skin for it to stay. His mark that can't be removed, until now.

The sight cuts into my oxygen supply. Looking upward, I don't know how much I can take of their love that only brings pain.

He doesn't move at first. He's just gripping the pole tight, not making a sound, cheek pressed to the wood that will taste his blood. Eyes closed, a twitch of his face with every descent of the leather handle.

With the next series of lashes, his head bangs against the pole. A grunt is heard, hands clasping together as he tries to breathe. His father doesn't stop. A full-grown wolf should know better. His offense has him getting the maximum. The silver will eat him today, will feast on flesh.

Kimberly makes it to the group, hysterical, screaming for her father to stop. Luna Catherine nods her head to someone as she's carried away, kicking, clawing. Her brother just looks at her.

"I love you," he mouths to her.

"No, no!" Her voice is a mournful cry, her arms outstretched as her body is pulled away. She's trying to touch him one last time.

The kiss of the whip's tongue ever so slowly fillets the words off his back. The love they share has ruined flesh. With each taste of the whip on skin, patches are starting to be removed, stripping flesh from bone.

The first cries are heard from his mouth. He drops on one knee, only to stand again. This time the rain of lashes do not stop; they keep coming and coming, until he can't stand any longer. His body is slowly giving out. He's crying now, full blown male cries of pain.

Bound hands try to break free of the chains, and the pole groans and creaks with the effort of him trying to get free. Fingertips raise to the sky. Is the moon kissing them?

"You know why this is happening?" the Alpha finally speaks.

"Yes," a quivering voice responds. The wind brings words from the past to the present, full circle justice for love.

Breathe.

I can't look anymore. This is too much.

"Watch." It's Dallas who is beside me. My hand grips his in mine. Does Clayton see how the tips of my fingers are turning white from lack of blood flow? Clayton tries to hold my eyes. He sees us standing there side by side. His head bows down. He understands.

Now that the screaming starts, he can't control it. The whip will always make you sing to the moon— it's not the song she wants to hear, but the song she has to bear. His body is withering against the lashes. His father's face is grim, and his mother is on her knees now, mimicking her son.

The ground is sucking in every drop, none to be wasted. His body sways now slightly, muscles exhausted with the effort of holding himself. He starts to slouch slowly to the ground. The punishment never stops. No more ink is left, nothing but red meat. No skin, it's been stripped bare.

The song of the whip is not music to my ears. Clayton's screams are getting quieter and quieter. Just grunts are coming out now as his body sinks to the barren earth. Nothing grows around the poisoned pole.

"You will eat last," the Alpha's voice rings out for all to hear. Clayton can't answer back.

Eyes half closed, half open, as if the eyelids are stuck in that position...I don't think he can blink any longer. He looks the way his moon looks, half dead. He's lying in a pool of his own blood. If the father doesn't stop now, he will die.

"Stop." I say it quietly to the night, to the pack, to the moon. He has taken enough. I can't help the word coming from my mouth.

Another pack member voices, "Enough."

Grumbling from the lower ranks, voices getting

louder with the need for this to stop.

Dallas takes a step forward. "Stop." He echoes my plea.

The Alpha drops the whip and walks away, different than when he came. Broken, smaller.

"Bring him." Dallas is already turning, walking toward the clinic. He's going to try and save his competition.

CHAPTER 15

Luna Made

The tree looks all twisted and barren without its leaves. Branches stretch up toward the sky. The moon's shadowy light makes it look hauntingly beautiful, even though there is nothing that makes them beautiful at the moment.

Bittersweet velvet warmth runs down my throat, distending my stomach. I feel bloated with the pain that his words caused.

The leading families have poisoned their young children's minds since birth against me. It's almost like a divorced human mother poisoning their young against a father who has done nothing wrong. By the time the young turn into adults, they realize what the mother has done, but it's too late for that relationship with the father to truly become what it could have been.

The Alpha is corralled with the Luna and Beta. All three stand shoulder to shoulder as the lower-ranked wolves prowl around slyly. Circling round and round, accusations fly out. The high-pitched voices of females ask, "How could you do that?"

The lower tenor of the males voices, "Low rank, what does that mean?"

Power in numbers, that's what I'm seeing. The alpha is the most powerful, but against a pack he is only as powerful as the lowest-ranked juvenile male.

Judgment time.

The low rank wolves make up most of the pack, while the higher ranks are a scattered few. If you have no faith in your leadership, then it's time for new leaders.

"She was a juvenile!" another low-ranked female yells from the gathering, a circle that's slowly tightening around them.

The moon in all her brilliance is watching. Stars flicker in the darkened sky, like candlelight in the wind.

The air is unstable as the pack presses into them. Males start to snap jaws, and females are moved to the back by males who don't want them hurt.

The illusion of them is wobbling as the light of their actions creates a new, brighter picture for all to see.

Luna Catherine looks at me, holding my eyes. What does she see when she looks at me? When I look at her, my Wild wants to come to the forefront. The constitution of me wants to challenge her; I want to right the wrongs she has done.

A crack of my jaw as it comes unhinged shakes my core. A howl lifts up to the moon from my throat that has never howled before.

My knee is the next to buckle as it shifts, molasses slow. Ripping the tendons, tearing the muscles, it realigns to its natural angle.

"No," I cry to the moon. I can't do this, not here, not now, not in front of these wolves to witness my second shift ever.

My wolf's eyes see different colors than I do. The wind blows now, rustling the fur that is starting to consume my naked flesh. Another shift of the opposite hip has me taking a position on all fours. Sinking my fingers into the earth, I beg it to give me strength. I can't do this. My shirt rips down the middle, exposing muscles that are liquid underneath flesh as the ribs shift into a ribcage of my true form.

Breathe.

The wolf in me is trying to tuck me inside her, trying to push me into the background as she ascends. Her eyes don't leave the Luna's now. A shoulder pops out of the socket with the weight shifting downward, back curving up, feet stretching, getting longer, higher arched, the shoes nothing more than tattered rubber. The wolf is in control now. A snap of jaw so loud has attention falling our way. Eyes that have never seen me are now seeing who I am…but who am I now?

"Her eyes," a female points out, as if just noticing my change now.

With great heaving pants, the rest of my body moves into its proper position until the only thing left of me is my mind, and even that the wolf now controls.

A wobble almost has my wolf face down before she recovers her quivering muscles. They have not been used in such a long time, it's like a new fawn finding its legs.

Justice, is that what she wants for years spent away?

As more wolves notice my posturing toward the Luna, they start to back away, letting nature take its course. Survival of the fittest.

"I won't fight you," she yells out to the wolf. The Alpha takes a position in front of her, protecting his queen.

Ears are flattened down. Intent is there. Nose pulls back, revealing the sharpened teeth. A paw takes a step toward in intended threat. The Alpha takes a step toward me, guarding the most precious.

Ridge fur rises up along the spine, puffing the coat of the Wolf up and out. The nature of my Wild wants to become big. Fierce. There are gasps from the crowd as they see something unusual. A sickness has been festering for too long, polluting the pack, making it weaker than it really is. Remove the cause, you remove the poison, letting everything heal.

Insanity.

Taking the first leap, my wolf meets the Alpha's jaws. He shifts like liquid water, smooth. The Wild is no match for a full-grown male. He shakes her neck hard before tossing her away like a rag doll. Blood on our necks tells us that he could have killed but did not.

The Wild doesn't stay down like his warning growl says. Instead, it shakes off the bite. Droplets of blood fly into the faces of the wolves, who are open mouthed. Shaking, the Wild is so full of absolute rage it pours off her skin in great waves.

The nature of my Wild is no turn tail. She meets the Alpha, head raised, teeth flashing. Tail straight, again she sees him not as her Alpha, but as something that needs to be put down.

What if she fails? Doubt creeps into me. She has no doubt as she lunges again. A shoulder opens up, causing a whimper and limp backward. Now it's her blood staining the dirt where grass doesn't grow, mixing with our mate's blood that has not dried yet.

The crowd is starting to shift, standing on my right and left. Wolves from my low rank stand together, safety in numbers.

The pack starts to nip at the haunches of the Alpha and Beta, leaving the Luna alone, saving her for last. She is our mother and should know better. If she could do that to her real offspring, what could she do to us? What has she done to us that we don't even know about yet? Real mothers don't do that. She is not worthy to be called Luna.

This is the pack's opportunity to cleanse itself, provide its own antidote.

Snaps, snarls, jagged teeth connect with the fur of leaders who are not leading as they should.

The Wild crouches herself in toward the confusion, trying to get closer to the real prize, the treasure. Another hard shake to the wolf's scruff has her yelping in pain again. He does not end us as he easily can.

My Wild lands on her side. He's rolled her so her stomach is exposed. A hard, severing bite to the tendon renders her immobile, the front right leg useless. The wolf still manages to rise on three good legs. More wolves start to flank us, nudging with noses to get behind them, trying to take the point from her.

Out of the corner of my eyes, I see the four brothers flanking Luna Grace. They are observing the power of a pack. Luna Grace is watching me in interest, her head tilting to the side, whispering something in her son's ears. A growl shakes the air from behind them. A lone wolf approaches the fight, stalking forward with menace. Black fur that can hide easily in the silent shadows, as dark as raven wings, makes its way toward the center of the action.

One paw in front of the other, he's just as big as the Alpha, except in my mind he seems bigger. Blue eyes of intelligence, a superiority radiates out, causing some wolves to tuck tail, crouching down as they back away. Eyes that put us under a spell, he's a perfect predator. This is his path, the alpha in him tittering on the edge. The moon's light now shines down on this show of ascension.

Ears tucked back, tail and head slightly down in a stalking position. Massive fur paws grinding out the ground underneath him.

He is elegance.

His head turns slightly to his family. They all nod in agreement to whatever he has said. Luna Grace looks bigger at the moment while Cash shifts into his fighting form, just as dark as the brother. Both of them are ready to deliver the remedy the pack desires.

The Alpha and Beta stand shoulder to shoulder, life-long friends that will go down together. Their swords are their teeth, and they use them now. Both brothers take running leaps toward their intended targets. Bodies collide, jaws ripping into flesh to expose bone. Luna Catherine screams in horror as she realizes you reap what you sow.

This is the second time she is on her knees this night, once for the son, the second for her mate. The wolf hops toward her, body stalking the best she can. The Luna pays her no mind, only watching and feeling every rip, every muscle that is coming off her mate as the new Alpha is slowly eating away at him, one bite at a time. The beta is broken flesh. Dallas picks his brother Cash as his new Beta.

Her head turns toward me, exposing her throat. "Do it," she cries out. Her position is held by hands gripping the ground where no grass grows. Her breathing is labored as she feels every injury her mate sustains.

"Please look after Kimberly. She's only a pup. She's not like me yet. Please watch out for her. Bring her up better than this." Her neck is all the way exposed, jaws clenched together tight. She's watching her mate die, pulling in his last breath as Dallas's wolf lets go of the neck. No surviving that injury, he's already dead now.

Jaws clamp down, not breaking skin because the Nature of my Wild can't, letting the Luna back away. This won't right the wrong that was done to me. This will only haunt us for the rest of our lives. Instead, the Wild turns her back, and the Luna begs to be sent to the moon. A streak of black takes the neck, ripping it away easily. Luna Grace doesn't believe in second chances. She finishes the Luna in

160

one quick bite and pull. Her muzzle is saturated with the blood of a rival. The Wild tries to back away from her, only stumbling on a paw that doesn't want to work properly.

She touches her nose with mine before bounding away.

A body presses into hers, cheek rubbing into our flank, up along our injured shoulder, a tongue trying to lick the wound better. His fur brushes along her fur. A soft gentle growl comes out of his chest into hers. It's a soothing, relaxing sound.

He presses the Wild down into a lying position, belly flat against the earth as he takes in the injuries, whining at the worst ones. A lip lifts, exposing teeth as he growls at the former dead Alpha. He's rubbing against my Wild, saturating his smell into the fur.

Without my consent, without Dallas's consent, the Wild in me marks him as hers. It's a quick strike to his neck. Dallas has no time to react. Small glimmers of thoughts start to penetrate our soul, wrapping around us like twine that binds us loosely together. She holds this wolf tight, not willing to let him go until we feel his sadness. That's when her jaw releases with a high-pitched whine.

Great pounding sadness washes against us as the last ties of his mate slips away from him. He wasn't prepared for that to happen. Dallas has been holding onto that last flicker of light for so long. Even after his mark faded, he still had that last little goodness to grasp on his darkest days.

Now I have ruined it, destroyed that last little bliss he has of her. He can never get that back. How can I be *forgiven?*

I can't breathe. What my wolf has done is unforgivable in my eyes. She starts to regress into herself as I make the shift from fur to skin. My arm hangs loosely at my side now. I get up, walking away from all this death and loss.

This is all my fault...

His eyes look like they could cry. His body is shaking slightly with the full loss. A sorrowful wolf song starts to rise from his throat, and his family follows his cries in mourning.

My mom's words come back to haunt me.

He can be claimed.

The dark hides my shame of what the wolf has just done to him, taking away his most precious gift.

He doesn't follow me. He doesn't say anything. It's his turn to hold onto the earth, fingers gripping tight to dirt that just crumbled in his hands.

His grief is too powerful at the moment. It's an epic loss that's hard to recover from.

CHAPTER 16

Love Hurts

My nose is above water, my lips below. The arm that's injured is on my stomach as my other arm is buoyant, floating beside me. The water's warmth surrounds me, while his cold, broken soul freezes my insides. Arctic waves of iced fury rock my foundation. It's a burning cold pain, dry ice steaming and smoking.

He's scorching and searing me with his anger.

What have I done?

The water only moves with my intake of breath, little waves hitting the side of the white porcelain walls. A hammer in my gut strikes hard. It's almost as if I can see the flash of steel on metal. I groan to myself. It echoes in this closed-up little room. I can only sense the most powerful emotions from him, but they are thundering loudly. I can't protect myself from their rumbling.

Our canvas is starting off now with the ugly colors, painted by me. Always I have the worst to *offer*.

My body rises slightly in the water as I inhale and sinks slowly down with the exhale. My arm hurts so bad that even with his ice hatred of me at the moment, my wound is overwhelming me. The water is the color of diluted cherry Kool-Aid. The wound still bleeds slightly. I don't care. Let me bleed.

Blackened ice is replaced now with grief's pain, its ivy circling around my spine, climbing up to my neck, constricting me tight. He can't breathe.

I'm not sure what hurts more: the complete hatred or the bottomless grief he's going through. I think I choose hatred; I can deal with that much better than his grief. It's as if he had the last photo of her face and I just destroyed it. Never will he have that picture again.

What have I done?

Love only hurts. The only love that I have known causes the worst kind of pain and destruction.

Sinking into the warmth, I just want to stay here.

He won't block himself from me. There's no bricked-up bitter room that he's hiding behind. He's letting me feel all of this.

Getting up, I sway with the pain. Good, let it sway me. I deserve this. I'm the lowest of the low, marking someone when I have a mate.

What have I done?

Why? I want to scream at the mirror. Instead, I whisper it—*why?*

The wolf is not understanding. She only feels bad for me. Not for what she has done. If given the opportunity, she'd do the same thing over and over again.

Drying off, I put on my robe so I can get to my wound easier. I put a towel there to soak up the blood still dribbling out.

A knock on the door has me taking little quiet breaths. A harder bang comes next, followed by a bigger bang.

"I know you're in there. I followed the trail of blood." I think it's Cash behind the locked door.

"We can do this very easy—you open this door up—or we can do this the hard way. I just come in." Before I even answer him, a hard crash creaks the foundations of the home.

"I'm coming!" I scream back. I leave the bathroom quickly before he decides to let himself in.

Opening it up, he looks around my small place. I hold my arm against my chest with my other hand. He takes a seat at my table, as if I just invited him in for a cup of tea.

"He sent me over to make sure you're okay. Let's see it." He motions with his finger to come to him. He stays sitting on the chair.

"No."

Well, it's obvious he doesn't like that answer by the hard line that furrows his brows.

"We can do this easy or hard. Your choice. I either see that injury or I make you show me that injury. I don't have the time for this or the patience." He's not the same wolf I met for dinner at his brother's house.

This wolf is *angry, mad,* and *raging*.

Just a second hesitation on my part is all that's needed for him to be up and on me. He pulls down my robe to expose the sliced tendon. It's a deep wound, meant to immobilize, not kill. His fingers poke around while I sway with blood rushing in my ears. My vision darkens slightly. He has to hold me up as I cry out in pain, my legs giving out underneath me. He supports my weight, sitting me down on the chair.

"I might get sick." I can't move, so he hands me a cup that's on the table. He just stares at me with eyes that aren't seeing me. He must be mind-linking with his brother.

"He says you should be fine. You need to rest and not move around too much. Don't come to work until Thursday. He'll have Aurora reschedule all your appointments."

Tears pooling from eyes that can't hold the salty water any longer, he looks up at the ceiling, exhaling a breath.

"Does he hate me?" His eyes go glossy again.

"At the moment, he's very upset with you."

"Tell him I'm sorry." I lay my head on the table, shoulders shaking.

"I'm not your go-between. I came here to check on you for him. Whatever else you two need, work out yourselves. I'm done. I have enough to deal with." He pounds his fist on the table, a growl tumbling out.

"How long!" His voice sounds tight in his throat while he sits back down on the chair.

"What?" I'm confused by his question.

"How long have they been together?"

"Since they pulled their first breath from their mothers' wombs." I see his jaw clench tight, teeth groaning in pressure not to explode in his mouth. He picks up a chair, throwing it against my wall. It goes through my drywall.

Love is hard.

"What did you do? Why didn't he claim you?" His accusations hit me hard.

"I wasn't her." Another tear rolls down my cheek, but he doesn't care.

"No, you're not her." Another fist pounds the table hard, the legs shaking underneath the violence.

He crosses his arms in front of him. He looks like restrained fury. Calm body, thunderous eyes.

Taking a few breaths, he sets the storms of sight on me.

"This just isn't right." He's growling out his words, still holding my gaze hard, his whole body vibrating with its own life.

"No, it isn't, but it doesn't mean you can make it right again." I can't look away from him.

"Your opportunity is now. It's what you do with this opportunity that matters. The past is gone, it's already been lived, and it can't be changed, ever. You have a choice to make." I give him stuff that I've read in some self-help books. Hopefully, this helps him. His body stills, eyes closed, and he pinches the bridge of his nose.

"What kind of wolf is she?" he says quietly.

This is my chance to taint it from the start, rub salty words into his exposed soul, but I won't.

"I never really knew her, but what I felt from others, she was liked. She had friends. She was

167

popular. She could make people laugh. She's beautiful. Her parents loved her. She doesn't have any siblings, the only child." He stares at the floor.

"She's loyal to the people she loves." That just hurt my heart to say.

"She's been as respectful to me as she could. It was only in the end that she wasn't what she was. She was twisting up inside. Made her say or do things that really wasn't her. She was as nice to me as she could be." He just sits and listens, holding himself just a little tighter. A sad look in his eye replaces the storm.

"I could smell her as soon as we got to the clinic. Can you even imagine what that was like for me, seeing my mate with her throat opened up?"

I just shake my head no. I feel as if this is all my fault. Guilt is building inside me. Do I have any silver in this house? It's just a fleeting thought.

"This male that I don't know pulls out his phone. He's crying. He's yelling into the phone, telling someone that Kennedy is hurt, they need to come, and it's all his fault. That's when I went after him, telling him she's my mate." His fist pounds my table again.

How much can this table bear before it breaks?

"He could have killed me. Do you know how that feels?" Instead, he just let me punch him once. Then he just held onto me, restraining me. He told me he was sorry, and in the end, he hopes he gets what's coming to him." Cash is visibly shaking again. The eye of the storm is done, and the tail end is coming around hard.

"I start to put the pieces together in my head,

everything that I heard about this pack. About him, you, her." Another fist pounds against the wood, shaking the foundation of the ancient masterpiece. The quality of workmanship stands strong against fists of iron. They don't make things like this anymore—strong, sturdy, able to take a beating, not bending from all the pressure.

Another pounding fist on the table and his knuckles split open, but the table remains upright. Some kind of emotion shadows in his eyes before he gets up.

He reaches into his pocket, pulling out two white pills. "He said to take them. They'll let you sleep." He goes to the sink, turning on the water as he looks into my cupboard for glasses.

"I'm not going to take them."

"Rya, either you take them, or I make you take them. Either way, you take them." He just stands there with his outstretched hands toward me.

"Cash, I'm not sure who you think you are—"

He's on me again, shoving the pills in my mouth, handing me the glass of water. Waiting for me to swallow. If I don't, somehow I think he will make me, so I swallow those pills down.

My injury opens back up, fresh blood saturating the robe's material. He takes some napkins, pulling down my robe to hold pressure on the wound, muttering curses to himself, to me, about the situation.

Swatting his hand away, I take the bloodied napkins from him. He sits there at the table and puts his head in his hands. He's lost in his own thoughts. A rumbling wave of anger rolls through me again from Dallas, but then there is this little gentle wave of pleasure now coming from him. I almost missed the feeling. I would have if I wasn't staying so concentrated on his emotions. That pleasure leaves quickly, replaced by guilt.

This medication is very slow to start working, but like a train that's trying to stop, my mind is slowly shutting off. That moving train is stopping in place. I can see how people love this, I think, laying my head on the couch, closing my eyes. I can hear the door open and close, but I just can't get up to lock it. I can't move, my limbs heavy as cement, anchoring me down into the couch.

Hazy drug-induced visions swarm. Who lit the fireplace? Did I?

A blanket covers me on the couch. My eyelids are just too heavy to keep open. Dallas's gentle voice is in my ear. "Go back to sleep." I do easily.

I'm being carried, my robe coming off my body. A low vibration of sound hits my body. I try to open my eyes, but it's hard to start a train that has completely stopped. It takes a lot of effort that I don't have at the moment. The medication I was given has left me useless, unable to even open my eyes.

I feel him pressed up against my side. His nose is against my neck, inhaling.

I can't feel clothes on him. All I feel is skin against skin. His mouth is on the spot that should be marked, pulling the skin in and sucking hard. I feel his excitement against me. I can't even moan, but I am excited by this.

"My mother says it would stay, says you're very

special, Rya. Should I mark you now, take your choice away?" He's over top of me now. All I can smell is his hunger for me. *Lick your lips good.*

This male wolf is rubbing his scent into my body, his cheek along my shoulder, trying to press as much of himself into me as he can. A growl, teeth scraping my stomach that will leave red lines. He's just above my hairline, sucking the skin there, leaving red hickeys in his mouth's wake. Everywhere he's touching me he's leaving behind a trail of red. He doesn't stop until all I smell is him all over my skin. You can't wash this off easily. It will need to fade on its own.

My eyes open to the low light of the morning. His head has left an impression on the pillow. His spot is still warm as I let my hand feel the fading heat. All I smell is a male's mating hormones all over the place. It's heavy on the tongue. It's impossible not to notice this pungent odor. It overrides every other scent on the body.

I'm completely naked underneath the blankets. I touch myself down below, thinking I feel like I have been taken. No blood, no pain when I rub my legs together. I am slightly wet when my fingers come out; my virtue is still there.

I get up. My tongue feels thick and dry. I can't swallow my own saliva.

Opening the tap up, I put some water in my hand and drink from it. As I wipe my chin, I look into the mirror. My breath stops.

What has he done? I have hickeys all over my body, along with teeth lines that have slid down my skin. I turn my body. At least he left my backside alone. My inner thighs, lower abdomen, and chest are littered with them. I check my neck; there are no claim marks. What did his mother mean his mark would stay? Did I imagine that?

I put on some very comfortable clothes; my arm still doesn't want to work properly. The white bulky bandage he put on it is held securely with tape.

On the table, there is a water bottle, a small medication bottle with a few pills in it, and a note.

We need to talk, just not yet.

That's all it says, nothing else.

He doesn't come back the next night or the next. He doesn't call me; he doesn't check up on me. When I try to call him, it goes to voice mail, so I stop trying to call.

There's nothing else from him anymore, no more iced pain, or raging grief, nothing. He's turned off the show.

When I walk into the clinic on Thursday, only my females are waiting for me. No other patients are there.

"Aurora, where's Dr. Valentine?" I finally manage to ask around lunchtime.

"He took the next two days off. Lots for him to do and figure out, he told me." I nod as if I understand.

"Rya, I'm supposed to tell you that he's hosting a pack barbecue, and he expects everyone to attend. It's Saturday at three." I just walk away, tending to the various pregnant females.

Friday has me finishing the rest of my paperwork

as the last patient leaves. I didn't see Kimberly this week. I will have to see what's going on and why she didn't come to a scheduled appointment.

A groan hits my ears; it's deep and full of pain. His cries stand the fur on end. He's slowly waking up for very short periods of time before they drug him back into a sleep of healing.

This is an example of why doctors are worth their weight in gold. What's supposed to have died, they are able to keep alive." Clayton's smell to me is of pain and hurt. Instinct wants to drive me to his room, but my mind keeps me away. He never came and helped me long ago.

Aurora's coming out of his room, carrying some vile-looking blood-soaked dressings. I see him then. His hands are restrained by thick leather attached at his wrists. He's on his stomach, sweat making his hair stick to his head. His lips are trembling, back exposed. He has no back; it just looks like ground-up meat. His eyes find mine, and I stop for a moment before he picks his head up and looks away from me. I can see his shoulders shake as if he's crying.

Pain like this has no peak. It doesn't stop in an hour; it holds your body hostage until you just wish for your death.

All this pain is because he believed in love.

"Why are his hands restrained?" I ask Aurora once she comes back.

"It's to stop him from tearing his own throat out. He didn't like that he woke up." My stomach drops. He thought that he probably would die out on that post. He never expected to live.

She closes the door behind her as she walks into the room. I can hear her low, soothing voice humming to him.

Friday night, he doesn't call or come over. All his hickeys have disappeared; it's as if he never marked me with his mouth. His scent is still inside my skin slightly, lingering, holding on in the crevices that can't be seen with the naked eye.

I go around back. There are giant bonfires burning everywhere, a giant pig roasting in the pit, along with tables spread out with food, lots and lots of food on display.

I brought two pies—lemon meringue. I was feeling slightly sour with the way he's just ignoring me, but that's my own fault, no one to blame but me. I just couldn't help but bring lemon.

I find him with my gaze. He's talking to several wolves. This looks the way an Alpha looks, the way he's holding himself as if he has the biggest balls in the woods. A smile touches his lips, and my heart picks up a beat.

His mother is calling me over with a wave of her hand and a friendly smile, taking me in the opposite direction of Dallas. I give her a small wave with my now-healed arm. I'm looking for my family, but I don't see them yet.

Luna Grace is standing at the picnic table that Cash and Kennedy are sitting at. She was released two days ago into Cash's care. Her throat's healing well, no more white bandages on them. I can't tell if his claim mark is there or not.

The scarring is extremely extensive.

She doesn't look the same, skinny, sunken in

cheeks, hair falling limply to the side of her face. No makeup, it's as if she just doesn't care what she looks like. If he's put a claim mark on her, she should be going into her heat next month. It's the weirdest thing to think about.

Could I really deliver her pup? The thought shakes my core values slightly.

She looks at me, and our eyes lock with each other before she looks away at the lake...anything but me, anything but Cash.

"Hello." I bow slightly to the Luna, giving my nice smile to the both of them that are sitting down at the table. No need to be rude.

"How are you feeling, Rya? I would have come to visit, but my son gave strict orders not to disturb you." She's looking at Dallas as he weaves through the crowd, touching members of the pack.

"Look at him. He's just coming into himself." The pride she has for him is evident in her voice.

When I do look at him, it's as if he's filled out more, slightly taller with a swagger of confidence, holding his head up higher.

A male Alpha who has come into his own, who's thriving in his new position of power.

Cash gets up off the picnic table, grumbling something under his breath. His mother gives him a snap of her jaw but doesn't say a word to him.

"Rya, would it be okay if I came to your house tomorrow? I heard Cash is going over to fix some holes in your wall that you have. I'd like to tag along, if that's okay?" She waits for my answer. I glance at Kennedy, whose head is slightly forward, hair covering her face.

"It would just be Cash and me. I want to watch him fix those holes properly. Drywall can be a tricky thing. You need to be patient with the drying process, and he's not a patient wolf." Tears drip onto the picnic table, wetting the surface slightly.

"That would be okay." I watch Cash bringing two plates of food. He sets both down in front of him with one fork.

"We're going to try this again, Kennedy." I can see how she trembles slightly with her name coming from his lips.

He pierces a watermelon with the fork, putting it to her mouth. Her head turns as she tries to slide away from him.

"Kennedy, remember what happened last time. You either eat this or I make you. What will it be?" His voice is restrained. His mother just looks on. My mouth is slightly open, not able to look away.

He presses it against her closed mouth, jaw clenched tight. He's quick pulling her hair back until her cry opens her mouth. He shoves the piece into her mouth, closing her jaw with his hands.

"If you spit it out, I will make you eat that piece again and again until you swallow it down. If you throw up what I feed you, you will eat it again." Her hands go around her stomach as she's rocking back and forth. He's re-programming new thought processes into that wolf, teaching her how to eat from his hand nicely. It's a long uphill battle he's waging against something that is so foreign to her.

She does swallow it down but then gags, throwing it up. He forks it up, forcefully putting it back into her mouth.

"Eat and swallow what I give you," he hisses in her ear, but his hand is gently rubbing her back. The pack is watching on, not saying a word.

"We have a different approach on this kind of thing, Rya," the Luna tells me, hooking her arm into mine as she leads me toward Dallas and a man who must be his father.

He has intense eyes of the brooding ocean. He reminds me of a Silverback gorilla as he strides toward us. Strong body, rippling muscles that can't hide underneath his clothes. Matured and aged, he is the most dominant here. I can't even hold my position as his eyes land on mine. I tuck my shoulders in slightly, wincing with a need to go down on one knee.

"Don't do that, Rya. Stand tall. Meet him eye to eye. He likes that challenge." The Luna holds her ground, giving her mate an appreciated once-over. Dallas walks side by side with his father toward me.

"It's nice that he came to the barbecue." I can't think of anything else to say. Words are leaving me as Dallas approaches, just staring at me now. His thoughts are raging inside of his mind. He doesn't bother to hide his feelings. Want is the one emotion consuming him.

"My mate would never miss this." She's smiling now to him as he approaches.

"What's going on?" I have a confused expression on my face.

"This is a mating ceremony. Didn't Dallas tell you about this, Rya?"

"No," I say, shaking my head and taking a step back.

Dallas is looking at me, his emotions saturating my skin with his need to claim me.

CHAPTER 17

The B Side

Squealing, giggling little bodies jump into the pile of leaves, tumbling the colors up in the air, so when they come down the leaves are scattered everywhere.

Dallas looks at me. His hair is warm and smooth, cut short at the edges with a little more on the top. Just a light trace of stubble on his face, as if he shaved late last night but not today.

"Whose mating ceremony is it?" I ask as Luna Grace looks toward Kennedy and Cash.

"Theirs." I swallow down the acid that climbs suddenly from the pit of my stomach.

"Does she know?" I regard Kennedy sitting on the picnic table being force fed by her mate. She's crying so hard that she can't even breathe. He just keeps on her. He's whispering in her ear, hand rubbing her back. He tries to rub her cheek, and she slaps it away. He holds that hand down while his other hand rubs that same cheek; all the while he's saying something to her. She regurgitates her food again, and he feeds it back to her.

"Yes, she knows." That's all she gets to say as the two males stand in front of us.

Luna Grace embraces that Silverback male. Cheek to cheek, he lifts her against him as if they haven't seen each other in a very long time.

"My female." He breathes into her ear, very low, pressing his nose against her mark. His teeth descend slightly.

"Not now," she says. He just bites her as she stills in his arms. He holds her like this, firm against his body, before releasing her with a gentle kiss to his mark.

"Do you feel better now?" Her voice is lower, and a flush appears on her face.

"Slightly, but I'll feel much better later." He gives her a very sly smile that they both must understand, because she returns it while Dallas looks away, uncomfortable. No one likes to think their parents are still having fun.

"Father, this is Rya. Rya, this is my father, Alpha Clinton." Hard eyes take me in from the bottom of my feet to the top of my head. He sniffs the air slightly. His eyes fall to mine, the muscle in his cheek twitches, yet I don't look away. I want to, but I feel firmly planted in my spot. Eye contact with an Alpha is very hard on a lesser wolf. Shoulders want to crouch, and you want to fall into yourself, turn your tail inwards with the dominance they exude. They smell different with more testosterone in their system. More of the Wild in them. I can sense the change that's happened with Dallas's smell. He's becoming more than what he was.

"Nice to meet you, Rya. My mate has told me a great deal about you. I'm looking forward to getting to know you better, along with your family." He doesn't touch me or shake my hand like a human. He keeps all contact away from me.

"Thank you, Alpha Clinton. Nice meeting you as well." He's looking at my eyes with a smile on his face.

"So it's true you are moon blessed."

"So I have been told." My eyes mean different things for different packs.

"Some would say that you are very special, that the moon has touched you herself." He takes a step toward me, inhaling again.

"So much of the moon's smell on you. My son is very blessed." He looks toward Dallas, who has his head down slightly. His emotions are swirling around from one to the other, and it's hard to choose what's winning out.

He still has my eyes, a turn of lip showing a slight fang. "You should really watch how you look into wolves' eyes, little moon. You need to be able to back up what you are doing." I cast my eyes to the ground, knowing better than holding an Alpha's eye for too long. It's as if I want to challenge them.

"Rya, I was hoping my mate and myself could have a talk with you and my son together alone to discuss this unusual relationship you have begun to form." The Alpha's voice is strong and vibrating against my chest.

"When she's ready," Dallas interjects before I have a chance to answer.

"That would be fine, Alpha Clinton. I know I have to answer for what I have done." I hang my head now with how shameful I feel.

"I would say your wolf has initiative. It's something you're born with. You can't learn it; it's just in you." He smiles to me gently, trying to calm the sweeping disgust in myself that I feel.

I see that Cash is dragging Kennedy away from the table, as her fingers are trying to grip the side of the wood, holding on as if her life depends on it.

Looking around, I see nothing special, no decorations, no balloons, flowers, streamers. Nothing that says this is a mating ceremony. It's as if this is not a special day. That no one cared enough to make anything really nice for the new couple. I see no presents on the table, no cards with money in a birdcage. Nothing around here that stands out, that this is something that means something to the wolves who are binding themselves together.

The female usually is dressed nice, with makeup and hair done, the male in nice dress pants and shoes. It's as if this is just thrown together half assed.

Cash is pulling on her hands as she screams for him to stop. He keeps at it until the last of her fingertip hold is broken on the wood. He lifts her up against him as her feet kick at his most delicate places.

"Stop." It's all he says as he pinches her ear hard. She stills with the pain. It's not meant to cause damage, just subdue with great pressure to the nerve ending. It's a very humane way to show dominance.

Once she stops her display of outrage, Cash leads Kennedy up onto the top deck. Pack members are gathered around like they are going to watch an outdoor concert.

Kennedy stands there looking solemnly at the lake; her eyes are only focused on that little island. Is she having memories about the little land in the middle of the lake filled with blueberries? Tears keep coming. She doesn't even bother to wipe them away from her freckled face. Hair blowing in the breeze gets stuck on her cheek. Her skin is pale, no longer sporting a healthy glow. You can see the pain and misery in her soul.

Her skirt moves in all kinds of directions as the wind slightly picks up. Her bare thighs are exposed, and Cash can't help but stare at them. Waves start to crash against the shore, the wind whispering a low moan through the forest as it bends the leafless limbs back and forth.

I can see Cash's strong pulse in his neck pound away, his hurricane inside himself blowing furiously.

He takes her hand in his. She pulls away, but his hold is too strong to break. The sun slowly sinks in the sky behind us, while the moon is rising above. The sky whispers a sigh as the last rays of light leave behind the darkened night that holds the moon in its place.

It's just Cash and Kennedy up there, no one else. Just those two holding hands, facing each other.

His muscles are twisting and shaking underneath the skin that wants to shed. She holds herself still, except her hands keep trying to break the grip.

An incantation of words begins to pour from his mouth.

"You are mine. You're my hope, my love, my light, my weakness, my strength." He pauses as if she is supposed to say something back to him. She keeps her mouth tight lipped, and I can see him eyeing her hard.

"You are mine. You're my hope…" she cries out on trembling vocal cords. He just stares dead into her eyes.

"My love." It looks like she can hardly stand up. Her breath is leaving her, the pressure on her hands looking like it's becoming unbearable. Her fingertips are white with the loss of circulation. He holds her in place, demanding her to say the words without him having to say a single word to continue on.

"My light, my weakness, my strength…" She's crying again, but it's not with happiness.

Dallas and his brothers stand with their parents in the front row of this show. I can't see their faces as they watch this beneath the moon's eye. I'm in the back, not really appreciating what this view has to offer.

This should be so much more, except there is nothing else. It's as if she isn't cared about. This won't be a memory she puts up on her wall.

Pulling her into him, he breathes in her scent. He makes a face of slight disgust; I guess those deep crevices in her skin still hold the lingering scent of another. That should all change now as he will wipe away all traces of him off her body. It's the mind that needs to be wiped clean.

He doesn't say anything else, and she tries to back away now. He's swift, sinking teeth into a neck that will never show his mark because of the other it holds.

A soft moan escapes her lips, her body wrapping around him without her consent. Nature taking its course, he ties himself to her. He staggers and almost falls as her essence slams into him. He sheds a tear; I'm not sure what for. He looks at her now as if really seeing her for the first time.

His neck angles to the side slightly, and he whispers something that makes her stiffen. It looks like some kind of threat. She shakes her head no. He still looks her in the eyes. "Kennedy, your choice, but either way I will be marked."

He turns his neck again slightly for her to have access to his throat. I wonder if she will open it up. His hand goes against the soft part of her throat, claws coming out, sinking into the flesh. She's bleeding slightly from it. I guess if she takes him out, he'll take her out, and they will both die together.

He pulls her against him so her mouth is on his throat. She's sobbing again, pounding at his chest.

"Do it, now!" She shakes her head no, but her teeth have descended. No one in the pack is making a sound. The wind is the only thing cheering them on as it rustles the leaves frantically on the ground.

With a heaving breath, she sinks her teeth into him, holding him to her. They stay like that for a moment, unable to move, cry...they are just breathing each other in. The moon is high in the sky, looking down at her children taking the proper path she has made for them.

This should be a beautiful sight we're witnessing. It's everything else but beautiful.

Isn't love grand!

She's unable to stand anymore, toes off the ground as he just holds her up, pressed flush against his body. I can smell him, male hormones of mating leaking out his pores, saturating into her.

Her teeth come out of his marked neck that is visible and red, still bleeding slightly. His claw comes out of her neck, and they both regard one another.

"Run." Cash's voice is deep sounding, his body starting to shift slightly to fur.

"When I find you, I'm going to make you mine in every single way." He lets go of her, taking a step back. Dallas looks at his watch and nods his head to his brother. Cash starts to take off his shirt, one button at a time. I think Kennedy is shocked, so much she can't even move.

"Will you make this easy for me? No chase." He's looking at her in the eye. Another button undone, exposing a smooth chest.

"You have one hour. I suggest you start running…fast." His shirt comes off as the rest of the buttons pop off, hitting the wooden deck. Her senses must have come back to her, because she starts to run, shifting smoothly underneath the moon, skin turning to fur fluidly. She's hugging the bank of the lake, her underbelly dripping with water as she runs like the wind to escape a mate intent on taking everything from her.

I have no doubts Cash will take her, over and

over again, until he's satisfied that only his scent creeps into every crack, every crevice she has.

The crowd disperses, seeing the show is over. It's much the same as our ceremony except there is no chase at the end. The mates walk willingly hand in hand off together, happily.

Dallas catches me looking at him. Can he tell when my eyes are on his body? He gives me a smile as he approaches. I don't return it, and his smile fades.

The wind has stopped just as suddenly as it came. The young are playing again, twirling around the yard, scattering the leaves. Torches are lit, sputtering flames casting shadows into the night.

"I would like it if you ate with me at my table," Dallas asks politely.

"No, I think maybe I should just sit at my own table," I say back just as sweet as my voice lets me. I hope he eats the lemon pie I brought. I made sure it was more sour than sweet. I'm still upset about not being called or even having my calls returned. Wolves who like each other don't do that.

He stands there for a moment, taking a breath.

"Rya, you're upset." Before I can answer, my parents approach us. I put on my best smile for them. Dallas stands beside me, his hand touching my back, fingers playing with the end of my hair. His hand slides down the curve of my spine until it rests on my lower back. I can feel his hand just resting there, innocent, while he speaks to my parents.

"Dallas, my mate and I were wondering if your family would like to come over for dinner?" My father seems so much smaller to me than I remember him. Perceptions change as you age; things you thought are not what they seem at all.

"My parents would like to meet with you as well," he says to my father.

My heartbeat stumbles slightly in my chest. His hand has a small tremor. I can't pay attention to anything that is being said. All I can feel is his thumb now drawing little circles underneath the material of my shirt. His skin touching mine is making my cheeks blaze with red. With a ghost of a graze, his other hand touches my jawline in a show of affection to my parents. They both are smiling their heart smiles that I don't get to see very often. His hand at the base of my spine starts to walk its way upward, touching every raised knob on my spine until his fingers are tracing where my hairline is at the base of my head.

My parents walk away with me not even able to say a word to them. I nodded yes or no, but that's all I could manage. It's as if everything falls away when he's near me now. I feel a pull deep in my soul toward him, not as strong as with Clayton, but it's there. A compulsion that needs satisfying.

"Please eat with me," he says low in my ear.

Wolves are milling around the food table. It's the meat that they're after, and no one can touch it until Dallas starts.

Platters and platters of food of every kind are on display…some I have never seen before.

He steps into my space, body pressed firmly into me, cheek to my cheek. His lips faintly touch skin.

"Please," he breathes. Pulling away, I'm left

slightly cold, the chill of the night air creeping in around my skin.

The remaining brothers, Caleb, Carson, and Crane, are carrying giant coolers. They open them up; they are filled with beer and other drinks. They have smiles on their faces as they each pull a cold beer out of the ice, looking at all the pretty she-wolves around them.

He takes my hand, leading me to the table of meat, handing a plate my way. He takes first, while I take second. The rest of the pack falls in behind us while we fill our plates up. Holding his plate in one hand, he leads me to his table with his hand resting low on my back. His spot is at the head of the table, and he motions me to his right.

Realization hits. If I'm at his table, Cash will be on his left, and I will always have to look at Kennedy's face. That makes me sick to my stomach.

I sit, trying not to hear the whispers behind me.

Standing instantly as soon as the whispers get louder, he looks at all the pack members.

"Does anyone have something to say?" He looks every wolf in the eyes, searching for something. He sits back down, grumbling under his breath. He's looking puffed out, a growl escaping his throat. He stands again, walking away from the table until he's in the center of the yard.

"Does anyone have anything they want to say? Speak up now." He's turning around, looking at everyone, challenging anyone to speak. No one says anything. Heads down, necks slightly angled to the side, they expose their throats in submission.

His father looks on with a smile on his face that scares the crap out of me. His eyes are starting to scan the crowd as well, looking for something that catches his eye.

Coming back to the table, he calls out to Cash, who's pacing on the deck. "Thirty minutes." I watch as he starts to shift to midnight black fur. Effortlessly, his change comes over him. It doesn't look like it hurts at all. Now the wolf is pacing from side to side, staring at the shoreline in the direction she went. His eyes are black to match his fur, his head up, scenting the air. He must have good control over the fur side of him.

The rest of his brothers take their places, his mother and father having full plates of food.

"What happens if he doesn't find her?" Now, I guess maybe I said something funny, because everyone starts laughing hard.

"He was trained by the best tracker we ever had," Caleb states. I take a closer look at Caleb; he looks like menace wrapped up tight in a skin's body. Chewing on a piece of meat, he's eyeing the crowd.

"My brother trained Cash. He could find anything or anyone." He looks proud when looking at Dallas.

Dallas just nods his way slightly with the compliment he just received. I feel his hand on my thigh, which makes me squirm slightly. He doesn't move it higher or lower. He just rests it there like it belongs.

Am I red again?

Emotions are strumming into me...his want, his

need, like vibrations on a guitar string that has just been struck. He's not eating anymore. I can feel the shadow of his eyes on my body. His hand moves higher up. I close my legs as my breathing becomes difficult.

I'm having a hard time trying to cut my food. My hands don't want to work as the wolf inside wants to come out and play with her mate. A whine is stuck in my throat.

"What does she want?" Dallas says as he has my face in between his hands, stroking my cheeks with his thumbs.

His eyes are all I see, the wolf's vision clouding mine.

"You." It's a muffled sound as my jaw is trying to realign.

"Rya, how often do you shift?" It's taking everything inside me to push her down.

"Twice." I can only get that word out. *Please don't embarrass me*, I tell the wolf as she tries to say hi to the party.

"Twice a week, that's not enough. You should do it more often or else you'll have problems like this." Luna Grace is talking to me like I don't know how it works, like I'm some newly shifted she-wolf learning the ins and outs of pack life.

"Mom, she means twice ever." It's Dallas who speaks for me. I watch as Dallas takes his watch off, handing it to Caleb. Everyone around the table is just watching me, and I'm mortified.

"No, that's not even possible," his father states, like he knows something I don't.

"Fifteen minutes," Dallas says as he takes off his

shirt and undoes his pants. My wolf progresses slowly, not as slow as the last time, but slow enough where it still hurts.

The elegance of his shift makes me jealous. I'm crude and monster-like.

His wolf is waiting with its back straight. My vision is changing along with my limbs. I fall away from the table on all fours, and a whine escapes out the wolf's vocal cords. It's her turn to stuff me inside of her, as if she's using her back legs to kick up dirt, she's kicking me away into the background, into the cocoon of skin.

Please don't do anything stupid.

The first thing she does is bite his neck again. The next thing she does is pee beside him, growling at the crowd, showing her teeth.

"Did you just see that?" one of his brothers says. I can't tell which one because things sound different. The pitch is all wrong as the wolf shakes her head.

The dark wolf gets up, sniffing where my wolf just peed. He lifts his own leg, saturating the ground with his own markings again.

My Wild has her butt in the air, front paws stretched out, wagging her tail as if she wants to play with him. He takes a slow step her way as she leaps into him. He rolls the wolf on her belly, nipping lightly before he takes off into the trees…the opposite direction Kennedy went.

"Three, two, one…go," his brother yells out to Cash, who jumps in one leap, clearing all the decks. His pace is fast, nose to the ground, hunting his prize.

Dallas's wolf is watching my wolf's approach at the edge of the brush line, tail wagging, tongue hanging out. He waits until we are just close enough before he runs away, looking back at us to follow. Running full speed now, he's beside her, pushing her forward harder and harder. Running together side by side. If she slows down, he nips her shoulder slightly until she goes faster. It's a very hard, long run, with quick turns, weaving in and out of trees. He runs her around a big circle. By the time we make it back to the party, everyone has left, a few stragglers carrying on singing by the fire. His brothers are entertaining females, guitars in their hands. The wolf is exhausted as she lays in the grass on her side, panting hard. He lays beside us, licking our jaw, our underbelly. She spreads her legs, and he licks us there, taking long pulls of air.

Imprinting our smell to him.

Before my eyes, he shifts himself back, laying on his belly in the grass. He's petting the wolf behind her ears, running his hand on the soft fur of the belly. He presses his nose against our neck. She gives him a soft growl of appreciation. She licks his face, and he kisses her cheek.

"Stay here. I'll get some clothes." He's firm with his command.

The party tables have already been put away, everything cleaned up nicely like there was never a party here to begin with.

The music sounds soothing against the wolf's ears as she throws her head back and howls her music along with the lyrics. The singing stops, and now people are laughing. She doesn't like the tone of the laughter. She doesn't like the way they are laughing at her. She takes a step toward them with a growl, raising her ridge of fur.

"Rya." Dallas is behind us with a blanket stretched out in front of him. The wolf turns a fang his way, but he's quick, grabbing her ear and pinching hard.

"Don't ever do that again." He holds the wolf there as she whines a sorry plea to him. She heels up to him with her tail tucked so far under her body I don't know how she's going to take it out.

"Shift." Without hesitation, she lets me ascend to break the cocoon of fur.

He wraps the blanket around me, handing me the clothes he brought.

"You can change in the house." He leads me away from the laughing people. I bristle toward them slightly.

"You change. I'll go have a talk with them for you. The bathroom is the first room on the right." He turns from me as he walks with tight fists toward his brothers and the females.

After getting changed, I can smell his room. His scent is so thick and powerful coming from that space that I open the door, taking a peek inside.

What greets me is something I don't want to see.

Looking around the room, I see pictures of them. Her eyes are always looking at him. They are always on his face while he smiles at the camera. Arms circling around waists and necks, lips touching cheeks. This is a shrine, and I'm standing at the altar.

A simple picture grabs my eye on his dresser.

Everyone always looks better in black and white, untouched by colors. You can notice every inch of them in more depth, except the eyes. I like how eye colors are hidden. My eyes in this kind of picture always look pure white. She's looking into the camera without a smile, just staring as if she were preparing for this moment. Her looking at me, while I'm staring back at her. We have a silent moment together. A future looking on the past.

I sink into myself. I have never been up on anyone's wall, on their nightstand, in their wallets, on their phones. Everything he's done he has done first before me. I get the second round. Maybe I'm meant to be the B-side, the last thought in someone's mind. Never really an option until plan A fails.

Another picture catches my eyes. A big heart is drawn in the sand, and their shadows are holding hands. Inside the heart is written **C + M.**

"You shouldn't be in here." Dallas steps into his room.

He's looking around at what I'm seeing. Something inside me breaks a little. I have a lot of questions at the moment.

I notice that there are brown cardboard boxes on the ground, pictures of them lining the bottom of them. It looks like he was in the process of putting her away in the closet.

I hit my hand on the dresser. I hit the other hand, causing my palms to go red.

I'm his B-side, the bottom row, the discounted item that no one really wants. I will always be this, no matter what. No matter who I meet, I will always be second best, the second choice, because I will never be anyone's first choice.

"Would you have ever not called her for a week? Would you have ever not talked to her for a day?" I ask. He looks away, guilty.

"I just want to know. It's just something I'm wondering about." I let my eye linger on their pure love, their happy love.

"No."

"Thank you." I walk out of the bedroom, out the door, and head to my car.

"Where are you going?" Dallas walks beside me, trying to touch my arm, but I won't let him.

"Home." Opening my door, I get in, but he won't let me close it.

"Are you mad because I didn't call you?"

"I'm mad at everything, I guess. I just want to be a thought in someone's head. A first thought, when you wake up in the morning. The last thought when you go to bed at night. I guess I just want to be a something other than what I am." I try to close the door again.

"Rya."

"It's okay, really…it's okay. I should be used to this by now. After all this time, I should expect this."

"Rya." He says my name again.

"Am I your first thought in the morning, Dallas? Do you think about me first?" This is going to hurt. I brace myself for it, holding the steering wheel tight in my grip.

"No." The tone of his voice is low, trying not to hurt my feelings.

"You were my first thought in the morning. You're what I think about when I wake up. I wish we were on my wall together like all those pictures you have up. I wish I just had one. Just one. Is that asking too much to want that? I tried to call you, left messages, but I guess I'm just not a thought that crosses your mind." I can't cry anymore; I can't feel. It's like I've been blessed with a blissful numbness now.

"Rya, it's not like that." His hand goes up, trying to touch my cheek. I just flinch away.

"I need to go. Tell your brother and mother to stay away. I don't want any of your family over at my house. It's the only thing I have that is mine, and even that is a hand-me-down." My voice remains monotone. I can't care anymore. "I have to go. Goodbye, Dallas." I can feel his emotions swirling inside him; he's afraid. The top of the food chain is afraid.

"Don't go. I was caught up in myself. I wasn't thinking clearly. I felt disgusted with myself, with this whole situation. I just wasn't prepared for it, to have her completely leave me. I thought I was, but when it happened, I wasn't prepared how it left me feeling." He's gripping the side of the door, kneeling beside my seat on the ground. His knees will be stained; everyone will be able to see that he has been on his knees for something.

"You made it very clear what you felt that night, the rest of the week. I felt everything you felt—the anger, the disgust, the grief, the pain—every single thing. You made sure I felt it, didn't you? You wanted me to hurt like you did. I'm so sorry she did that. It wasn't my intention. I never meant to take your choice away."

"I just couldn't come around you. I would have taken your choice away from you. I want you to be with me because you want to, not because I forced you to be. That's why. I couldn't deal with everything happening all at once."

"You could have called me, said something to me. Anything is better than nothing. Do you think I deserve nothing, Dallas?" He bangs his fist on the steel body of the car. Why do the things I own get dented, destroyed by others?

Why do I allow my belongings, myself, to get destroyed while I sit back and just watch, being a spectator at my own destruction?

CHAPTER 18

A Chase

The light from the car's interior illuminated his eyes in the spectrum of blues. Electric wavelengths of emotion pulse living thoughts into my body. This is how it is between mates: they can feel the other's thoughts. If I were to mark his skin side, I could be inside his body with my mind, not just feeling his strongest feelings.

"You deserve so much. You deserve everything. I was wrong for doing that to you."

He curves his hand around my neck, pulling me toward his face. It's paralyzing the way his eyes hold me, the way his thoughts drift to my neck, wanting to just take.

"To tell you the truth, the honest truth, I was afraid to recover from her. I wanted to keep her inside my soul, keep that last little connection I had with her. Until you came along, I never had to face the fact that I needed to really say goodbye to her. I was fine with waking up every day feeling nothing.

I was fine with that. Get up, brush my teeth, put on clothes, eat, go to work, come back home, go to bed, get up the next day, and do it over and over again. I was fine with that." My hands are still clenching the steering wheel. His fingers are working underneath mine, breaking the hold I have on it.

"Now you make that not fine. You make me feel things I never thought I would feel again…you make me feel alive." One finger slips off the steering wheel, and his other finger works the other one, but he's looking at me the whole time.

"Do you know I could smell you before I even walked into the clinic that day? I stood outside the door debating whether or not to come into the clinic. I felt sick with how I was betraying my mate, thinking how amazing someone else could smell." His fingers just broke the grip I have on the steering wheel; he holds my hands in his. His fingertips brush against my knuckles.

"I was packing her away, Rya. That's what you were seeing in my room. Finally packing her away, not forgotten, because I could never forget her. It's time for me to recover from her and start living my life again." Baby blue eyes plead with mine for understanding.

"I need to be accountable for my actions. What I did was not right. I should have called. I never realized by not calling you that this could be our defining moment. I can't have this be what makes you turn away from me. With my mate, I just knew how she felt. With you, I'm blind. It's not an accusation. It was a dick move on my part. I

200

apologize for that."

The touch of his hand on my hip travels up my spine.

"You made me feel really bad about myself, about what I did to you." I try pulling my hands away from his grip, but he won't let me.

"Don't feel bad. You forced me to live again. I had to grieve. I needed some time. When you felt my anger, my disgust, did you also feel my pleasure, my hope, my desire? It was there in the background, but I need to go through the bad stuff first, get over it so I can really just focus on the now, what's important now." He brings my hands to his mouth, and he's kissing them, putting them against his cheek, rubbing his scent into them.

"I'm not sure, Dallas, if—"

"You're not sure? It's too late. Your wolf marked me as hers. I can tell now when you're looking at me. I can feel your eyes on me. Do you know how long it's been since I felt that? Do you know when I'm touching you like this I feel as if you're mine?" I notice the way the hair on his arms are gravitating to my body, just like mine gravitates to Clayton's. He's feeling the pull now, my wolf's mark binding him to me.

"My wolf's going to claim you soon, Rya. I need you to be prepared for that. I won't stop him. Your wolf has claimed him, and he needs to do the same." I can actually almost see the emotions playing behind his eyelids. It's the wolf in him that's making it very clear what he wants and needs. My wolf tries to ascend slightly to meet the wolf's eyes. She wants us to be taken; she wants to be chased.

"Please, Rya, just give me a chance, just a chance." He's looking at me the way I was looking at Clayton, a desperate pleading in his voice.

"That's all I'm asking, for now. I know what I did was crap, and I'm so sorry, because I can see in your eyes that you couldn't care less what I'm saying to you now. That I really don't matter anymore. I can see that you're ready to just walk away and not look back."

"I just don't know."

"You marked me, Rya."

"I know."

"I can't let you go, I can't just let you walk away, and I won't recover from you." He's dead serious. "You're the first female that I have kissed since her, that I want to rub my scent into, that I want to protect even before you marked me. I wanted you without the mark. We've both been through trauma, both of our situations so different, but trauma nonetheless. We have both faced it alone. Maybe it's time just to take a chance on something that can be so good." My mind is back and forth on that pendulum swing riding up and down.

"I wish I was in your head so I know what you're thinking right now," he whispers in my ear.

"I'm just not sure how to feel."

"Well, I'm sure. I'm going to do my best to wait till you're sure. The wolf won't wait, he's not going to wait, but I will try my best." He's getting off his knees now. They're stained with muddy dirt that will be easily cleaned off in the wash. No lingering stains for wolves to see he's been on his knees.

Lips press against mine, slow and soft, before he pulls gently away.

"I'm going to close the door now. I'm going to let you drive away now, but tomorrow I'm going to be at your door asking to come in. I hope you'll let me in, but if you don't, I'll come the next day and every day after that."

He closes the door, the interior light turns off, and I drive away from him.

Passing the clinic, I see Kimberly outside of the clinic doors.

Parking my car, I get out, looking at her. "Kimberly, are you okay?" She keeps her head down, not looking at me, just walking away without a word.

"Wait, Kimberly." I try to touch her shoulder to stop her. She spins on her heels; her eyes are so red and puffy, they look almost bruised and swollen.

"They won't even let me see him! I can't even see my own brother!" she screams.

"What do you mean, they won't let you?" My voice goes up a notch.

"They said I can't see him." She holds her little belly, and I know for a fact she's gotten thinner, and she has a duskiness to her skin.

"Come with me." I pull her by her hand into the clinic. The lights have been dimmed for the night. I have never been here at night; it feels different, quiet.

I'm met in the hall that leads to his room by Aurora, her arms crossed over her chest, an angry expression on her face.

"I told Kimberly that she can't see her brother yet."

"Why? It's her brother." I take a step toward Aurora, gripping Kimberly's hand as I try to push my way past her. Aurora doesn't budge.

"He doesn't want her to see him like this...not yet." Aurora voice holds a softness yet a firmness that his wishes will be maintained.

Kimberly is crying again. "He's my brother. He's all I have left. Please, just let me see him. I promise I won't do anything bad. I just want to see him...please." Aurora still stands firm, arms crossed over her chest.

"No. I'm sorry, Kimberly. He's my patient, and I will respect his wishes. When he says you can see him, I'll call you."

"Kimberly, stay here." I slide past Aurora as she turns to me.

"Did he say that I couldn't visit?" I tilt my head to Aurora.

"No."

"Well, maybe if I just went in and asked, maybe he'll let her see him."

"You can try. I'm not sure if he's awake. I just gave him something to settle him down. He's not doing well at the moment, Rya."

"I'll be quick. If he says no, then I'll leave."

Opening the door to his room, I don't want to smell him, but I do. I smell his pain. It's sinking into my skin. The hair on my arms start to tingle, and my neck tickles with how he affects me.

It's hard to look at my poison, how he's lying in the bed, belly down. His arms at his sides, but still in thick leather restraints.

He looks innocent, without sin. Closing the door behind me, I take a step closer until I'm at the edge of his bed. I can see how he shifts slightly in his sleep to get closer to me. A moan escapes his mouth, and his body quivers slightly.

His back is still bleeding; those white bandages are stained with fresh blood soaking through to the surface. He's pale, his lips tinged blue. After all this time, I still feel as if I could lean down and kiss him. Just one time, kiss his lips and feel what that would feel like. If it would feel different than kissing Dallas.

My hand goes on his head. I just can't help myself.

Deep-seated compulsions slither into me like a snake hissing urges into my ear. I let my fingers touch his hair—just once, I tell myself. I just want to feel what his hair is like.

As soon as I touch his head, his eyes open. I pull my hand away quickly. I let it hang limply at my side.

"Am I dreaming?" He doesn't take his eyes off me.

"No." I can feel those pine green eyes on my skin, looking everywhere until they fall on my face. This is how Dallas feels now when my eyes touch his skin.

"I have Kimberly outside. She needs to see you." He shakes his head no. Grimacing with the movement, his jaw tightens, his teeth clench. A little small groan escapes the base of his throat. He looks like he's in misery with the pain.

I could soothe his pain, I could run my fingers through his hair, and I could just sit next to him, and I'm sure it would ease his suffering somewhat. That's what mates do; they're supposed to ease your suffering. Only my mate has made me suffer for years, and never once has he tried to ease any of my suffering.

"She just wants to see you. She's young and needs to know her brother's okay. I think it would help her."

"I don't want her to see me like this. Rya." It's my turn to shiver slightly.

"I can put some covers over you, hide all this from her so she can only see your face. That's all she wants to see." He takes a few breaths, his eyes closing as if he could fall back asleep.

"Please, Clayton." His eyes open to find mine. With a nod of his head, he gives his consent.

Pulling up the covers, I hide all the damage that has been done to him. As I pull the covers over his restraints, his fingers find mine, gripping my hand. He's still strong. Energy shifts from him to me, me to him. He doesn't let my hand go, holding onto it with just the tips of his fingers.

"I can smell him all over you." His teeth try to descend but can't in his weakened state.

"Now I know what you went through smelling her on me. I can't even imagine how strong you are. I'm only beginning to understand what I've put you through." I break his grip and cover his hands up.

"Rya, just release one of my restraints. I just need one off." He has a pleading voice now.

"No, Clayton, you know why I won't do it,

because I don't forgive you." Turning my back, I leave the room.

"Aurora, he said it was okay."

Waiting outside of the room for her, I give them privacy they need. She comes out after fifteen minutes, looking better.

"He fell asleep. I'm going to go. Thank you, Rya." She doesn't look at me when she says this, just tries to slip by me. I grab onto her arm, pulling her into my office.

"I just want to examine you real quick. You missed your appointment, and I understand why." Leading her to the table, I encourage her to lean back. Lifting up her shirt, I spread the cool jelly on her lower abdomen and turn on the ultrasound.

She turns her head from the screen. Taking measurements, I record them down to compare to her last visit. He's very tiny—active, moving around everywhere—but very tiny. This is not normal at all, and Dallas will have to get involved in her case because she is so high risk for a c-section.

"Don't you want to see your pup?"

"No."

"Why Kimberly?"

"Because I just don't." She gets up without even wiping away the jelly, just pulling her shirt down and her pants up.

"What's going on? You can talk to me."

"No, I can't. I want to talk with Kennedy, but he won't let me get near her."

"Who, Cash?"

"Yes, Beta Cash. He's insane." She means what

she says. The look in her eyes tells me she must have had a run in with that wolf.

"How about I talk to him, see what I can do? If that doesn't work, I'll talk to the Alpha, see if he could talk to his brother." She just stares at me, open mouthed.

"Why would you want to help me?"

"Why wouldn't I?" She has no response to me. Instead, she turns around, walking out of the clinic.

"Do you need a ride home?" I call after her.

"No," she yells out.

"Are you at your house?" I call after her so I know where to look for her if she misses another appointment.

"No, I'm staying with my mate's mother." She doesn't look happy about it.

"Is your mate here now?"

"Yes, he's back. No sense him staying, he can't afford the tuition for next semester anyway. My father was paying for him to go to school. Now he's back looking for a job." She just starts to walk away from me, head down, looking so lost and sad.

"Let me drive you home."

"No, Rya. I just need to be by myself."

Getting back into the car, I drive the rest of the way back to find my yard a mess. Trees that Clayton knocked down still remain toppled over on my beautiful garden; my door is still gouged with claw marks. Walking inside, there are holes in my wall. Everything is just a mess.

Nothing to do but start cleaning up everything in the morning. It's a hard night of tossing and turning, insomnia at its best.

The knock has me jumping out of the shower, putting my hair in a towel, and wrapping a robe around me. I find Dallas standing on the other side of the door, a little smile on his face. I stand at the entrance, blocking the path inside.

"I wanted to ask if it was okay if I came in, just to talk. Have some morning tea." He's holding up a bag of loose leaf tea. I can smell blueberry leaves and mint.

"Brothers," he says loudly as his three brothers round the corner. They look as if they've been in a very bad fight.

"You have something to say to Rya."

Caleb takes a step in front of the other two brothers, as if he's the spokesperson for the three stooges.

"Rya, we're sorry for laughing at your wolf last night. We just never saw a wolf try to sing before, and we thought it was funny. We were wrong for laughing." All three boys' heads are bowed slightly to me.

Looking back at it, I think it probably was funny to see a full-grown wolf sing a song.

"She doesn't like to be laughed at."

"We're very sorry. We never meant to offend her or you." Caleb sounds very truthful, no wobble in his voice.

"They're here to help clean up your yard. I thought maybe you could use a hand." Handing the tea to me because I haven't moved to let him in, he grips my hand, pulling me into him, so I'm outside my home with him.

"I'm going to clean up all this mess, Rya." He

209

places his mouth along my neck, sucking in my flesh, marking me with one of his hickeys he loves to do. It will fade by tomorrow, but today, if anyone sees, they will see I have someone interested in me.

"Once I'm done out here, my wolf wants to play with yours. I won't hold him back any longer. If she wants, he could chase her down. You could get a head start and we'll track you, but when we find you, we get to claim the prize." Without a second thought, my wolf ascends. It's not as bad this time. It's faster with just a hint of pain along my hip bones as they shift and pop into place.

She sits there just staring at him, head tilted.

"Go, I'll find you." With those words, she takes off into the early morning hours, excited to be chased down by her male.

CHAPTER 19

Conflict

Leaves that have seen better days crackle and break underneath my wolf paws. They look like candy, brightly colored, scented so sweet she tries nibbling at them. Giant pines look like guardians of the forest, standing up straight, protective, virtuous. Pine-scented earth swirls around us as the brittle needles are disturbed.

The land still holds the soft spice of autumn and its harvest that is almost over.

Dallas finds my Wild playing in the undergrowth, trying to hunt up a mouse. I sit back inside of my wolf while she discovers her nose. One trail a dead end, the next trail holds a better promise of finding something to eat that tastes better than leaves. Her nose sticks to the ground, paws now drenched in mud. She has forgotten about the chase she was promised. Instead, she's focused on her own hunt.

Glancing his way, while her nose is pushing

away the dead leaves for that trail she's still on, we never even heard him approach. How long has he been watching?

She greets him with a softly wagging tail, playfully jumping on his back, only to scamper away and do it again. His tail swishes back and forth, and my wolf is mesmerized by it as she tries pouncing on it. Back and forth, his tail plays with my wolf. She's stalking the tail as if it's prey. Jumping high in the air before trying to pin it down, she tries to take a bite out of it, but she just isn't fast enough to catch it.

She's makes loud, rasping growls from the back of her throat when that tail escapes her mouth. She went for his ear with her next leap, biting down with a tight, clenching jaw. He whimpers, backing away slightly. Lightning fast, he strikes her ear hard. She whimpers until he lets go. His growl was intimidating to her as she slightly crouches in on herself.

He licks her jaw, pressing his cheek against hers.

His nose to the ground, he starts to rummage around, scattering the debris of the forest floor until he finds what he's looking for. Clamped in his jaw tightly, but not dead, he holds a squirming mouse. He clamps down slightly harder, injuring it, but not killing it.

Dropping it on the ground, the little mouse drags its body, willing itself to get away. My wolf sniffs it, picking it up in her mouth, dropping it back down on the ground. He's watching us, not moving, just looking on with a tilt of his head.

The struggling mouse tickles my wolf's tongue.

When she crunches down and that first trickle of blood saturates her taste buds, it's magical tasting meat for the first time. Crunching bones in her jaws, she swallows it down, looking at him, the provider of her food.

My Wild starts to nuzzle him, lick him, brush her fur against him. She is in awe of this wolf who can provide food for her.

Setting off on the trail of meat, he hunts up several more mice, letting my wolf make the kill. She's getting gluttonous, drunk on the blood of living creatures. His wolf takes off fast and hard on a trail of something, nose to the ground. His fur is iridescent black, blending into the shadows of the forest where the light doesn't penetrate. He disappears in the undergrowth for moments at a time.

My Wild waits, sitting on her haunches for him to come out with another mouse. Instead, he comes out with a rabbit, placing the dead animal at his feet. He takes a stance over it, watching my wolf as if waiting for something to happen.

She's in a greedy mood, wanting that rabbit between his legs for herself. As she approaches him, he bristles his fur, a malignant growl tumbling out of his throat. She gives him her own menacing growl from deep in her throat. Nose wrinkling, she shows her teeth to him, and he does the same back to her.

One paw takes another step toward his kill, her shoulders crouching down, tail straight. She postures her intent to take what he wants to keep. Another snarl for her not to approach, but she doesn't listen to his warning. Her teeth almost sink into the flesh of the rabbit that is still twitching slightly in death.

A sharp slash of teeth opens her ear up, and blood starts to drip onto the leaf-littered forest floor. He takes a step back over his kill, waiting, watching her. The consuming hunger that rages in her stomach makes her forget the consequences. She half circles him with lifted lip, exposing her teeth. He pounces on her threat instantly, pinning her to the ground. He just holds her there until she stills underneath him; the threat of spilling blood from her throat of life is real in her mind.

Getting up again, he stands over his prey. My Wild doesn't move off the ground. He snarls once more before tearing into the flesh, consuming the meat bite after bite as she watches him. Swallowing when he swallows, licking her lips when he does, she doesn't try to move from her spot. He tosses her the remaining half of the rabbit. She crunches it down between powerful canines. She like rabbits more than mice.

Crouching down on her stomach, tail wagging happily, she gives him her peace sign. He gives her his own as he starts to lick her jaws and nuzzle her neck. Rubbing down her flanks up the other side of her body, he throws a leg over the top of her back, making to saturate every inch of her in his smell. She welcomes it from her provider of meat.

Her posture to him is of consent. Her neck angles to the side as his nose presses against where his mark will go.

She whimpers to him, a sing-song voice of a

wolf wanting to have a mate's mark. He's a provider of food; he can be the provider of all her basic needs and her pup's needs when the time comes.

He's a male of worth.

Gripping her neck between powerful jaws, he presses down, sinking teeth into flesh, and our world comes alive.

He steps away, and blazing blue eyes observe us. Pain deep in our spine drops us to our belly; legs can't hold our weight. Creeping tentacles of warmth overtake the pain. Slowly sliding in is a velvet bond taking hold.

Heartbeats croon to each other, trying to sync to one rhythm. It's a matchstick flame that's starting between us.

The ebb and flow of emotions pound inside me, a rupture in my soul being repaired by a new bond taking hold. I feel great guilt to Clayton, great agony as a small part of me is being ripped away violently.

The Wild in me is beyond satisfied. Her mate is beyond anything she thought possible. She is looking toward a future with this wolf as I try to let go of a mate I had no physical connection with.

Strong fingers rub down the length of my wolf's back, down her thighs, behind her ears. He's whispering soothing sounds to her and me. He understands this; he's felt the same thing. He knows the severing of something that's embedded deep inside.

"Shift for me, Rya. I want to talk with you." So on the forest floor surrounded by the decaying rot of fall, I shift, meeting his eyes as his lips brush against mine. So soft, so gentle, so comforting. He's holding me against him in his powerful arms, fingers gripping into the flesh of my hips.

"I can feel you. I can sense everything you're feeling now. The guilt, the pain, the pleasure, and the conflict you're having inside yourself." He sounds sad saying the last part.

I just lean my head into his chest, letting him cradle me against him. He brings me in even closer as he holds me, not letting go as I sink inside myself with drowning emotions of back and forth thought. Guilty pleasure consumes me, and I weep into his naked flesh. Part of me feels like I'm draining out, while another part feels as if I'm getting fuller.

Rough strong hands grip me tight, and shivers run along my skin from his touch. A moan comes out of my mouth, he brings me into him even closer. He's between my legs, my back pressed against the dampened ground. Looking into the sky, I see those dark green pines, standing, watching, swaying in the wind. The scent of pine in the air swirls around my nose.

"Rya." The maleness of him wants inside his female, to join as one.

He holds himself there, not moving further. Stiffening underneath him, I'm not ready yet for that.

He understands without words.

"Let's go back to your house." He's up and off me. I look at him, all of him. A male who's in prime physical shape. Desire pounds into me. He throws a smile over his shoulder before shifting effortlessly.

His midnight wolf rushes me before turning at the last minute into another direction. This entices my Wild to rise within me. The shift is not so bad now, not really fast, but much faster than before. We play a teasing game of chase all the way home with him leading the way. She couldn't get herself back home yet; she has no idea how.

The late stage of the afternoon sun greets us as he shifts, opening the door for me to get into my home. I notice how my yard is all cleaned up, trees chopped down, the wood stacked in neat piles for the next winter. If I try to burn it now, it would just smoke and really not produce the heat that is needed in those long winter months.

Dallas stands outside the door with clothes in his hands that were placed right beside the door for his return.

Making it to my room, I shift into skin, getting dressed quickly. Taking a quick glance in the mirror, I can see the mark on my neck that his wolf placed. It's a faint scar that tells others that I have a male who has claimed me as his. It's not as bold as when the skin side marks you, but it's still there, letting all the wolves know to stay away. No males like their females touched by other males; it causes battles of the dying kind.

So now we will see if all those tales are true of a moon-eyed wolf being able to hold marks of other males, not just their true mate. All the stares I received when my eye color finally took hold when I was away from here. That pack's Luna paying me a special visit, asking questions that she had no right asking me. She was very interested in how my own mate rejected me; she only had daughters, no sons. After that, there was always a Luna trying to meet with me for this reason or that. I was offered numerous job opportunities in other packs, but their offers were all turned down by Luna Catherine.

A memory filters across my mind. Have I met Luna Grace before? If I did, it was two years ago. I need to ask her about this.

Looking at my mark, I feel as if this will stick. It doesn't hurt, it doesn't itch, and it feels pleasurable as my fingertips brush against it. My eyes flutter closed slightly, the effect of touching the mark causing a fire to spread inside me. Desire, want, a need start to build up within. Undercurrents of deep pleasure start to pulse to life; goosebumps raise and shiver the surface of my skin.

"Rya, can I come in?" Dallas calls from the door where I left him.

Coming out of my room, I see him standing at the entrance, waiting to come in. He's dressed, a slight blush against his neck. He's breathing slightly harder, eyes that want, his emotions screaming to take what's his now. A male Alpha wanting to have a Luna by his side.

"Come in." He takes that step inside my home, relief inside himself felt within me.

"Do you regret it, Rya?" His head is tilted slightly, waiting for my answer.

"Yes and no." It's my truth that I need to tell him now.

"I understand. It must be very hard for you."

"It is, and it isn't. I know that Clayton doesn't want me, but deep down inside me, there was hope." The look of hurt in Dallas's face hurts my soul. He grips onto the chair as a wave of fear passes over him that I will choose Clayton in the end. It's a painful hurt that he's feeling like his stomach is being sliced open with claws, letting his insides tumble out.

"I'll fight for you, Rya. I will fight for every inch I gain in your soul. I'm not going to give up on us."

"I'm sorry, Dallas. It's not what you wanted to hear, but I can't help how I feel." It's almost like those abused women who would prefer to stay with an abuser than leave and have a better life. That's what I see when I see Clayton. He has never wanted me, he has never shown me love, yet deep down I want him in a very sick way. Yet here's Dallas standing in front of me, trying to be everything that I need and want.

"I'll just have to work harder, won't I, to change your mind?" He's getting closer to me now. His body warmth encases me with a feeling of fullness instead of emptiness. "I've been talking with Clayton, making sure that he knows everything that's happening between us, between my brother and Kennedy. I've been keeping him informed of everything. I think it is easier for him, so nothing is a surprise when he does fully heal. He has all day to think about what's happening. He has nothing but time as he heals to deal with all of his feelings toward Kennedy and my brother. He never expected to live. Do you know what his biggest concern is?" His truth will hurt me just as much as mine hurt him.

"His first words out of his mouth when he woke

up was, *is she okay*. He wasn't asking about you. He only wanted to know about her. He doesn't care about you, Rya. He also gave me his blessing to mark you, to make you my mate." His words take my breath away, and my stomach feels just like his, ripped open and bleeding.

"This is not meant to hurt you, but I know it does, Rya. Clayton and Kennedy were my friends before you came back. They would pick me up, and I'd go out for dinners with them, hang out with them on weekends when I wasn't working. I actually like that male. They were a fun couple. I asked him once how could he fight the mate bond. Clayton said it was easy. You weren't around, and he loved Kennedy. That you just weren't what he wanted, that you were not his type of female. When he said that, Kennedy would interject and tell me what you looked like. How you were really ugly with big teeth, no shape to your body. She said that you had no friends, that your family wasn't from good stock. You were prone to aggression. That you tried to kill her when you were younger." He shakes his head to himself. "How you were whipped for that. That they had to stand there and watch. She thinks you did that on purpose just to make Clayton feel bad that you got whipped. You should have seen the shock on their faces when I said in my pack we would have let you fight it out. Winner gets the prize. We don't whip our juveniles. We let them fight until one submits to the other."

"If I could have fought her, I would have won." I say it with a conviction. My Wild would have drunk at her throat of life.

"I have no doubts that you could take her back then, but now, I don't think you can. She is a female who has spent years training by Clayton's side. Learning, watching him. You might be bigger, stronger, but she has more knowledge about fighting than you do. Try to remember that." He's trying to make his point, staring hard into my eyes.

"My brother has to sleep with one eye open. She has tried many times to open him up. She's very eager to show him all her skill she has learned at Clayton's side."

"She's tried to take your brother out?" I'm slightly shocked. I thought maybe she would succumb to the bond.

"Yes, she has. I feel very sorry for my brother. He's got the biggest heart out of all my brothers." He's looking out the window, his attention on the shoreline. I notice Cash walking barefoot in the water, looking at the ground, eyes sweeping down where water meets land, little rippling waves soaking the bottom of his pants.

"He hasn't found her yet?" I ask.

"Not yet, seems she gave him the slip for now. Used the water to hide her scent. Very smart wolf he's dealing with. He just needs to be smarter than her." I watch Cash. He's slowly walking away from our view, hands in his pockets, looking at the waterline for clues.

"He's insane," I blurt out.

"No, he's just hurting, probably worse than her. I think he always imagined that his mate would fall at his feet. It's hard if your mate is in love with a wolf of greater power. He feels inadequate against

221

Clayton. How can he compete against an Alpha? He's of alpha blood, but he isn't as strong as him, and that's hard on a male wolf. You females look how beautiful another female is; males look at how powerful another male is." He's sitting on a chair, looking around the room, looking at the walls that have no pictures hanging on them. A blank canvas of white that I really need to paint with colors that I love.

"Are you afraid of Clayton?" I'm curious of what he thinks of my mate.

"No." One word spoken with a conviction of feeling that I know is his truth. He reaches his hand out for me to take. I do, and he pulls me on his lap, so I'm straddling him on the chair, feet dangling, not touching the ground.

We sit there in quiet for a while. I'm in my own thoughts as he just watches me. His face changes slightly with the emotions I'm feeling. How can I hide what I feel from him?

"Have I told you that you smell like blossoms on a fruit tree in the springtime? Do you have any idea what you do to me now? I can feel inside of you, Rya." I see the hairs on my arms now angling toward him. He's affecting me on a primitive level, my needs, my wants, my desires. He gives me a low growl that makes my body respond naturally to him. I can feel the little sparks of electricity that run along the length of my body, pooling into my lower abdomen.

His hand gently brushes my hair, bringing the ends to his nose as he takes in the smell. His other hand rests on the curve of my hip. I kiss his neck, his ear, his jawline, rolling my body into his. His hands go up my shirt, finding flesh that wants to be touched. I moan into his mouth as the door bursts open.

I jump off him. We see Cash carrying Kennedy in his arms. He's soaking wet, as if he's been swimming. Her lips are blue, barely breathing. She smells cold. Her heart rate is very slow, her breathing very shallow and slow.

"Put her on the couch, Cash. Rya, light a fire. What happened?" Dallas is in complete control of the situation as he assesses her.

"She's really cold. How did she get so cold?"

"I found where she was hiding, that island in the middle of the lake. She must have seen me and tried to escape. Just plunged into the water and started to swim. I couldn't get her into the canoe. She overturned it." His teeth are chattering, and he's shivering with how cold he is.

"So we started to swim back together. Midway, she just started sinking in the water. She started panicking that she was getting too cold, that she couldn't make it. She said her muscles were starting to cramp up." I notice Dallas's hands start to shake slightly. Some kind of memory flashing behind those eyelids—fear.

The fire starts to rage in the fireplace, not hot enough yet to produce the heat that they need. I get my duvet from my bed, putting it on the floor next to the fireplace so that they both can lay on it next to the heat. I will have to burn it afterward; I can't stand her smell.

He picks her up as he lays down. With her back

223

facing the fire, she's pressed tightly against him. Covering them up, I get a spare pillow for their heads so they can share it. I'm going to burn that as well.

"She'll be fine, but you can't move her until she warms up," Dallas instructs his brother.

"You need to be careful around the water, Cash. How many times have I told you?" Dallas raises his voice, and Cash winces slightly away.

"I know, Dallas."

"No, you don't know! You could have died. She could have died!" He's full-on yelling at him.

Turning away from them, I have to do something other than gawk. I decide to start on the soup while Dallas keeps yelling at his brother. Going into the little cellar, I gather up the root vegetables that I have saved in wooden crates. Taking what I need, I make my way upstairs. Filling a big pot of cold water, I put it on the stove. Hot soup to heat them from the inside out. I can't believe she's in my home. The wolf grumbles she doesn't like her; it takes a certain kind of focus to clamp her down inside me. She wants to have a nice short talk with that female.

Cash is looking my way. "Get that wolf under control or I will control her for you." His words are a threat that riles up the wolf's fur.

"You need to be able to back up that look, Rya. You can't, so put her away." Cash's voice is harsh against my skin. She looks like a beautiful sleeping doll in his arms. No wonder my mate loved her. I could never compare to that.

"Cash, enough! You won't be touching Rya, or

else you will be touching me. Do you understand?" Dallas leans over his brother, exposing his sharp teeth to prove how serious he is.

Dallas pulls the covers up over them more, so only their heads stick out. He pats Cash on the head like a good little dog.

"Rya, they need to stay here for just a little while...until she wakes up and can move. I'm going to my house and grab clothes for the both of them. I'll be back very soon, okay? I need to stop off at the clinic anyway. Cash, behave." Dallas leaves, giving me a quick kiss on the forehead.

"I'll see you in less than an hour, okay? I know this is difficult for you, but sooner or later the both of you will have to try and get along."

"I don't like this," I say, not happy with being left with an insane wolf and *her.*

"I know, but you're the better wolf, Rya. Remember that." He leaves with a brief kiss on my mouth.

The soup is coming to a boil. I turn it down to a simmer. This should be good for them, especially her if she hasn't eaten in a while.

I hate that they are here, but I just can't turn away someone who is hurt, especially a female.

As her hair dries by the heat of the fire, I notice those beautiful sun-kissed highlights are fading with the oncoming winter. I fill up the fireplace with more wood. She stirs in his arms, opening her eyes. She's looking into his chest, then around the room.

Her eyes fall on mine as I stand above her. They look tired, uninterested as she unfocuses them. Her mouth is a straight line, her smile a memory. The damage that love brings hides in the shadow of her neck. Up close, I still can't see his mark that he has placed on her.

This is his second-hand treasure that he holds tight against him. She was already treasured by someone else; he just let go of it for someone else to claim as theirs. I wonder if when Clayton gets better, he will try to reclaim his golden ticket.

She falls back asleep against his chest.

I can't smell that he has taken her yet. She doesn't smell like that yet.

"What are you looking at?" He watches as my eyes travel the length of them.

"Why are you doing all this to her? Why not just let her be with him? She doesn't want you."

"The thing is, Rya, I'm not a quitter, like you. I just don't give up on my mate." Looking at him funny, I'm somewhat confused.

"I did try to fight for him. I have the scars to show for it." How dare he say I didn't fight for him? I tried.

"One time, you tried one time only. You got your hand slapped and decided just to quit and give up, hide away and cry yourself to sleep at night, feeling sorry for yourself. Did you try your best, Rya? Did you put all your effort into your fight?" He huffs out his breath, already thinking he knows the answer.

"You left him, walked away from him, and didn't fight for him. That's how I see things. See, that's the difference between you and me, Rya. I won't quit. I will wake up every day and fight for what I want. It's not easy. It's a lot of work." He brushes the hair out of her eyes, kissing her forehead. "I will put as much effort as it takes for us to be together." He looks down at Kennedy, who's sleeping peacefully in his arms, exhausted from being out for so long.

"Rya, you just gave up on yourself. You just gave up when things got hard. You decided that it was too difficult to fight for something you wanted. You just couldn't see the light at the end of the tunnel. I see that light, and I will do everything I can to reach it for her, for us. This is where she belongs, by my side." His teeth have stopped chattering; the slight blue tinge is gone.

"If you hurt my brother in any way, I will tear your throat out myself. He's a good wolf, Rya, better than anyone I know. I'm not sure that you deserve him." He turns his head away from me.

"He needs someone who will fight for him. He's not that same wolf. I'm hoping he will come back to us the way he was. Can you be that wolf who brings him back?" I'm not really sure what he means by that, so I don't respond.

Watching, Kennedy snuggles into him more. She whispers, "Clayton," into Cash's neck. Instantly he stiffens, shaking her awake.

"If you dream of him, you don't get to sleep!" he yells into her ear as she jumps, waking with a crying scream.

Such a twisted interpretation of love.

CHAPTER 20

Just A Nudge

The tension is so heavy at my table, tongues are talking, tense through gritted teeth. Chairs squeak as we shift positions uncomfortably, trying our best to get comfortable.

I am unable to stop myself from looking at Kennedy, up close and personal. I'm just trying to see what she has that I don't possess. What's so special about her?

"Stop staring at me." She doesn't look me in the eyes as she opens her mouth for Cash to put the spoon to her lips. She takes what he offers, except I am the one who provided all of this. I hate the way the metal clinks against the porcelain bowl. I can't look away as he takes another spoonful, blowing on it before putting it up for her to take another bite of my food.

Cash gives me just the slightest glare. I still don't turn my eyes from her. I just can't stop staring. The way her lips are full and thick, the way her hair falls in soft curls around her face, the way her chest gently rises and falls with each breath. I just can't stop wondering about this female. What makes her so much more than me?

"If you don't stop, I'll make you!" Now her eyes are on mine. My wolf is excited by her threat.

Dallas has his hand on my back, rubbing in a calming, circular motion. It works, slightly.

This is a nightmare come true for me. I would have never predicted this, ever. Kennedy sharing my food at my table. The next thing is me helping her ease a pup into the world. I won't be able to do that. I can't be expected to do that.

Already I can detect just the faint change in her scent; the way she smells is ripe. She will have to start changing her panties regularly now. Her body is producing more fluids for her male to smell. Instinct and hormones are at play that can't be controlled. Her mind will rebel, but her body is full steam ahead. Cash will become a force to be reckoned with as her heat progresses. Aggression takes over. A need to matc and producc offspring will be all-consuming to the both of them. Enemies becoming one in an age-old dance.

How will she feel after this? How will she meet her lover's eyes when she has her mate's pup in her belly?

Love is hard.

A knock on the door has me greeting Luna Grace and her Silverback male. He's something else as I let my eyes travel the length of him.

He's sophisticated, well-aged with a look that he can belong anywhere he desires. You make room for him and adjust to him and his needs.

He smiles toward me as I try to get myself under control. The wolf in me wants to stare at his eyes, a compulsion so great that I can't pull away. She thinks she is her equal and doesn't want to turn tail toward him.

"Rya, enough." His voice is deep, with a slight menace of threat below the layers.

Luna Grace, watching the interaction, says nothing, just observes her male and myself.

Dallas is quick to stand beside me with an arm around my shoulder. His body just angles slightly in front of mine, protectively. He pushes me very smoothly behind him. His father laughs slightly, and the mother gives him such a sweet look as if to say, "That's my boy."

"It smells so good in here, Rya. Is that soup you made?" Luna Grace steps inside. She's looking around. Her eyes never stay on any one spot for too long.

"Are you hungry? I have lots left."

"That would be wonderful." They take a seat at the end of the table as Dallas sits at the head with me on the right.

"How are you two doing?" Luna Grace is all smiles, waiting patiently for one of them to answer.

"How do you think we're doing?" Cash spits out.

The alpha's big paw of a hand lands on his son's shoulder; he's showing teeth. "No need to speak like that to your mother."

"I didn't mean for it to come out that way. I apologize." Cash's voice is very soft now. Kennedy doesn't look at anyone; she just keeps her head down, trying to hide behind the curtain of hair.

Putting the bowls in front of Dallas's parents, I'm feeling very awkward.

"Rya, do you have bread? This would go very good with bread." She dips her spoon into the soup without scraping the side of the bowl. She eats silently.

Taking a deep breath, I get her the bread she wants.

"Kennedy, would you like a piece of bread?" Luna Grace says.

"No." She says the word very low in her throat. Cash rubs her back as she shakes slightly.

The relief I feel inside me is beyond heaven. Never would I break bread with that female.

I feel as if I'm just waiting for an implosion to happen.

When Kennedy lifts her eyes up, they are of a she-wolf who wants to tear into something. My nails bite into the palms of my closed fists.

A low growl escapes her chest when her eyes find me. A flash of teeth from her, as mine, say hello.

"They need to work this out." I hear the Silverback male putting his two cents into the conversation that Kennedy and I are having without sound. Actions sometimes speak louder than any words.

"It wouldn't be fair, Father. She hasn't trained. She can't even shift properly yet." Dallas stands up, coming once again beside me.

"Maybe I should teach her." Cash and Dallas both look at their father in surprise.

"No," Cash answers for me.

"Why not, Cash? Afraid she will be able to back her teeth up once I'm done with her?" his father says very quietly. How is it he can project strength in a whisper?

"Father, I can train her." Dallas speaks up to his father.

"No, I think you would be too easy on her. She has too soft of a look. You would give in too easily." His arms cross over his massive chest.

"She's needed here. She has a few females who will be birthing soon."

"You deliver them. You're trained for that kind of emergency." His father seems like he has an answer to anything Dallas can throw his way.

"You know how I feel about that. You know that it's hard for me." Dallas's voice gets low and very serious. He's prickling up his back fur along his spine. I can feel how tense Dallas is becoming.

"I'm not going anywhere with you." My turn to voice my opinion.

"Rya, I could train you to become what your wolf wants to be. She would be able to back up those sharp teeth instead of tucking your tail underneath you. You need some guidance that you never had. I could help you."

All of our heads turn toward Kennedy, who starts laughing at me. I can taste the vileness in it, the bitterness she feels. The wolf in me hates when wolves laugh at me. It makes her insane. I throw the bread I'm holding at her face and actually hit her. Crumbs scatter on the table and floor, sticking to her head.

Implosion.

She clears the table easily, in one massive leap.

Before I know it, I'm thrown into the door hard by hands that are reaching for my neck.

"Let them do this. They need it," Luna Grace yells out to the two males, who are now trying to separate us. Cash and Dallas let go and slightly posture to one another before their father rumbles his dislike for that.

My fist connects with Kennedy's jaw; I think my hand hurts more than her face. She takes the punch easily with a smile full of sharp teeth. It looks like she can take a punch as she begins to laugh again.

The Alpha gets up and opens the door, taking us females by the scruffs of our necks before throwing us outside. It's as if he has done this several times before with how smooth his actions are.

Landing on the ground, Kennedy rolls on her side, springing up faster than me. Her fist answers mine back with a bone-crushing crunch. I think she broke her hand on my jaw that is now hanging off its hinge.

A kick to my stomach makes me gasp, another kick comes, but I grab her foot, twisting hard, making her fall down. I'm on her with fists that fly hard at her face. It's like high school all over again. I wonder what the watching wolves are thinking.

Kennedy is crying her rage, pulling my hair back. A knee to my back bruises delicate kidneys, an elbow to that side of my jaw has me dizzy with pain. She takes the advantage as her fists land again on my face. She rolls me off her, so now I am the one on my back. She straddles my chest, and both her hands wrap around my neck, squeezing the life out of me. I can't take a breath in as my hands try to break her hold.

The Silverback Alpha pulls Kennedy off of me, kicking and screaming. She's thrown at Cash, who catches her easily in his arms.

Dallas is encouraging me to take big breaths into my oxygen-starved lungs.

Cash is looking at Kennedy as she circles around him, posturing to her mate that she's not happy.

"Stop touching me!" she screams to Cash, who stands straight. Her words hurt.

"You're not him. You have no right to touch me. How could I even find you worthy when I had him between my legs? You're nothing compared to him. You are nothing but a weak little wolf. You can't even begin to satisfy me the way he does." Both Cash and I flinch at the acid dripping from her voice. "When he gets better, he will challenge you for me. He will tear your throat out, and I will eat your heart while you lay dying at my feet." Her laugh bubbles out of her mouth as if she is also on the verge of insanity.

"He doesn't want you, Kennedy." Cash's voice is calm, cold, as he regards her. He circles her so she has to spin slowly around to face him. Is he still going to try to put his effort into her? It seems she doesn't appreciate his fight. "He gave you to me. He threw you away, like garbage. I would never have given you to anyone. He doesn't care anymore." His canines have descended.

"He loves me! He's going to fight for me. You're a liar! He would never do that to me!" Tears once again are coming down her face, which is bright red and starting to bruise.

"I'm going to teach you, Kennedy, who you belong to. It's not him. You're my mate, and we belong together. I know it's hard for you, but I won't give up making you understand this. I'm going to make you understand who I am to you." He grabs her, biting down on her neck, hard. She moans from the contact. Her body is the biggest betrayer her mind will ever know.

Hands wrap in his hair, their bodies melting into each other's. They hold that position for just a minute, unable to untangle themselves. Reason must have found her brain as she begins to kick and scream, but he restrains her from doing damage.

He wants to be her oxygen, but she's refusing to breathe. Unfortunately for her, she's going to be forced to breathe him in.

"You both need to leave now!" Dallas is in front of me, hands cupping my cheeks, shaking his head sadly.

"At least you tried, Rya. You might not have won, but you tried. No one likes being laughed at. Maybe next time, she might think before she tries to laugh at you. She knows now that you will fight back." His fingers caress my bruised jaw, tucking a stray hair behind my ear.

He brings me into his chest, where the smell of him envelops me. It's alluring. His touch soothes my pain. I feel the thrum of his body with my presence so close against him. My heart rate starts to slow, trying to match his. He just holds me tight and safe against his chest. No one can touch me now in this minute. He wouldn't let that happen. Fingertips are now at the curve of my neck; my jaw feels better pressed against him.

"Both of you go. Cash, you should take her to go see him. Have him tell her himself if she doesn't believe you. Remember, Cash, you can't hurt him. He's injured, and it wouldn't be a fair fight. It would be without honor for you to hurt him when he can't defend himself." His words are thrown like knives against him, sharp and to the point.

Kennedy actually perks up. Her bruised face still is beautiful, and I want to hate her for that.

I'm not sure that I'm prepared for the next family dinner. One day, maybe we could all sit down like one big happy family that you see on TV. For now, our dinners will always end in violence and bruising instead of hugs and kisses goodbye.

Dallas takes my hand, leading me back inside. He sits me down on the chair. Looking inside my freezer, he gets some ice in a plastic bag and wraps it in a towel. Handing it to me, he starts to clear off the bowls of half-eaten soup. Placing them in the sink, he washes them.

"Are you okay, Rya?" Luna Grace asks, taking in my injuries.

"I'm fine." I'm slightly ashamed I'm not a good fighter. I deliver babies, not fight for the pack.

"You put up a good fight for not being trained." She pats my leg, rubbing it slightly. "You females really need to try to get along if you can." She says it like it's the easiest thing in the world.

"I've seen you before, haven't I, Luna Grace?" My jaw barely moves with my words because of the

236

pain. I just need to change the topic of conversation.

"Yes, you have, Rya. I was never really introduced to you. I've seen you before in the pack that you were trained in." Her big male puts an arm around her shoulder.

"I heard a rumor that there was a moon-eyed female training away from her pack, so I had to come and see for myself." She leans into his arm, and he kisses her temple.

"You see, Rya, you're very special. That mark on your neck won't fade. You are the only one born in a century to carry the eyes of the moon. You have a choice. You get to decide who you want as a mate. Imagine that, the moon giving someone a choice." Her smile reaches those eyes that look so loving. Even my own mother doesn't have eyes like hers.

"Are you upset with the choice the moon made for us?" The Alpha smiles into her neck before kissing it.

"No, my male, I'm very pleased with her choice." He runs his fingers through her hair, and I need to look away from them. I'm embarrassed by their outward display of love. For them, it doesn't seem that love hurts; there is no pain in their faces when they look at each other.

"As I was saying, I have never been introduced until I arrived here. My sister is the Luna of that pack you were at. She called me, knowing that I would be interested in someone like you for my son. She told me your mate rejected you, that you were available for the taking." Her words sound truthful. She looks me in the eye, never looking away.

Dallas sits down beside me, arm over my shoulder, a kiss to my neck. His mother smiles at us approvingly.

"Go on, Mother, I'd like to hear the rest of this." I put my hand on his thigh. His muscle quivers from my touch.

"I never approached you personally, Rya. I wouldn't do that. I did help my son decide about this pack. There were many offers on the table for him. He was wanted by many. I told him that I had a good feeling about this pack, that maybe he might find something of worth there. He was on the fence at first. The pack is small. So I mentioned to him he could do it for only three years, give it a chance. We set up a contract. If he didn't like it there, he could leave after three years. I also had him put in the negotiations that if he found a potential mate that he is free to bring her back here. That she would be allowed to leave the pack to go live where my son decided if he didn't want to stay. The former Alpha of this pack signed it without question. Imagine my surprise when they told me the contract was not going to be honored."

"Is that why you pushed so hard for me to come here? You knew she would be coming here. How did you know that I would take interest in her?" It's obvious he's feeling slightly betrayed.

"How could you not take interest in her? She's the most beautiful female I have ever seen, inside and out." I turn red with the compliment.

"So what I did was just give you a nudge in the right direction, my son. Just the tiniest push to see if anything could happen between the two of you. If you weren't interested, then you weren't interested. No one was forcing you to like her. You did that all on your own. You liked her on the outside first, but I bet once you got to know her, it's the inside that made you like her more." She's waiting for his answer.

"You're very right, Mother." He's looking at me closely. Everywhere his eyes roam, I can feel them on my skin.

"I'm happy that you are giving my son a chance to prove that he can be what you need. He's a good wolf, Rya." She gets up and presses her cheek against his. "We are very proud of him."

Dallas sits still, his emotions whirling inside him. He's trying to clamp down on his feelings, not letting anyone see how her words affect him enough to shed a tear that doesn't come out.

"We should go, my male." Standing, they walk toward the door.

"Rya, consider my offer to you. My hand is always extended your way if you need to take hold of it. I can train you so your tail will never curl under. Imagine that, Rya, never having to be a turn tail to any other wolf besides my son." A gleam in his eye twinkles out before he turns his back on us, closing the door.

The next thing that Dallas does is walk toward where the blanket and pillow lay, picking them up so I don't have to touch them. He opens the door, heads to the fire pit, and throws it in to be burned later.

He's brought a big bag with him. Opening it up, he unfolds his duvet that only smells like him. "I brought you this. Hope it's okay? You can sleep with it now." He sits himself on the couch with his feet up, legs spread.

"Come here, Rya." I do as he tells me.

Making myself comfortable between his legs, I press my hurt jaw against his chest. Placing his blanket over the top of us, I lift my shirt up. He tickles my back; strong fingers with just an edge of nail grazes up and down the length of my exposed skin.

It feels so good to just have caring hands on my hurt flesh. My body melts into his, as if it's meant to be this way.

"When you went to the clinic, did you tell him that you marked me?" His hands stop roaming skin.

"Yes." His voice drops low.

"What did he say?" My breath holds in my throat.

"He was conflicted. He understands what's happening to you. It's the wolf that doesn't understand."

CHAPTER 21

A Chance

Saturday night turns to our Sunday morning.

The air is chilly, yet inside the covers, it's warm and comfy. His body is hotter than mine. Dallas stirs gently, the music of his breathing gentle against my neck. We're cuddled in close, my thighs, knees, calves curving around his.

His arm is around my waist, while his other arm is underneath the pillow we're sharing. I run my fingertip over his braille vertical scar on his forearm. I feel the rise of the healed skin, the impression of the silver meeting flesh that will always leave its lasting mark.

He tries to pull his arm away, but I won't let him. Continuing to feel the scar, I bring it to my mouth, kissing it, running my tongue down its length. Once I'm done, he laces his fingers around mine as his thumb circles my own.

"Good morning." His voice is sleepy soft. His lips find the back of my neck, gentle and sweet.

"Good morning," I say back to him as I push myself closer. His hips press against my bottom, and he curves himself into my spine, his bicep flexing as his muscles shift his weight, so now I rest easily underneath his body, my back pressed down in my bed. His tongue teases flesh; desire pours heavily off his skin, mine leaking out and wetting my dark green panties that somehow have managed to stay on my body. Never once did he try to pull them down.

His boxers remain on, the fabric getting wet from my body's reaction to him. Nimble fingers trace just underneath my ribcage. It's a slow rhythm he's using with his hips, positioning himself between legs that part just a little more for him to keep the firm pressure against me. Rubbing, gliding as I close my eyes, biting down on my lower lip. Legs wrap around behind him just under his ass, heels digging in to press him into me more.

Lips are touching where my moan is coming out of my throat. My excitement builds low in my belly.

"I did promise that I would leave these on, didn't I?" Those words are pressed against my mouth. He's got his finger on the outside of my underwear, stroking a nail up and down on the fabric.

Shivering in pleasure.

"You said something like that." My voice doesn't sound like my own; it's lower than normal. He teases the spot that wants to be touched the most.

Eyes the color of light blue quartz regard me. They look as if they are getting lighter, like mine.

His clawed nail pokes a hole into the thin

material just under the waistband of my panties, a faint sound, almost as if scissors are cutting through the cloth. His nail pulls down, creating a slit in the fabric from front to back just under the bands holding them up.

He slips a thick finger inside me, and my lips part in *bliss*.

"We'll keep them on like I promised." He says this against the spot where he could mark me if he wants. His scent is changing into something more potent, more male. It urges my hormones on to kiss his skin, taste him with my tongue, nip with my teeth.

In and out with the ease of a practiced musician, he plays my body like strings on a guitar, making me hum inside myself.

He throws the covers off of us, and my smell swirls around the room, thick and heady. He looks down between my legs, parting them more, spreading me wider for his eyes to take everything in.

"You're mine, Rya." His proclamation drives my wolf wild. I moan as he pushes his finger further inside me, but not all the way to tear my virtue.

He leaves that intact.

Dipping in and out, he playfully teases me.

Sucking the skin on my neck, he lowers his body on the bed so he's at my chest, capturing each mound in his mouth, twirling his tongue to elicit moans of pleasure from me. His finger never stops its perfect rhythm.

He slowly moves down, kissing just under my ribs, pressing his nose into my soft belly, inhaling deeply. My hands fist into his hair as his fingers continue playing my melody that makes me sing out loud. Head thrown back slightly, I arch into his hand, wanting more that this male will bring to my body.

I feel coltish nerves as he travels still lower down my body, my thighs quivering, trying to close together, but wanting to stay open.

A sigh escapes out my open mouth as the first flick of tongue meets my most feminine part. He brings me into his mouth, tongue *velvety good*.

Sucking me into him, as those fingers play inside me.

On my own accord, I spread myself more for this epicurean savoring what I have to offer him. Nectar leaking out of me that he greedily laps up. He seems to be enjoying himself, judging by the vibrations from his chest I can feel through the mattress.

Fire burns inside me like shredded kindling, burning hot and fast throughout my body.

Another gasp from me draws his moans out. His one hand grips my pleading hip, trying to hold it down as I begin to squirm slightly, new intense pleasures taking hold inside me.

Lifting his head up from between my legs, he just looks at me like I am the most beautiful thing he has ever seen. He's feeling such desire it's pounding the inside of my body like giant waves against a break wall.

He's also feeling very blessed.

His head dips back down, devouring me like a connoisseur, tasting in the delight of me. I never realized how a tongue can give such pleasure, was made for pleasure.

I close my eyes as it begins to be too much, natural instincts taking over. He keeps his fingers inside me as I start to squeeze and pulse around them. Toes curl as my body stops momentarily, paralyzed with a rush of deep, mind-blurring ecstasy. Moans escape my parted lips until my back arches, mouth opening partially while I give a moaning cry out.

This is going to leave me quivering for days.

Looking down after the waves subside, I have painted his shoulders, neck, and scalp with my claw marks that line his skin.

The bedsheets are now embedded with our mixed scents. He nips at my inner thigh before placing a soft kiss to each leg. Another kiss is placed against the apex of my legs.

Panties are in ruins, but they remain on, just like he promised.

My breathing has yet to return as he trails kisses up my body, leaving little reminders he was there. My wetness saturates his boxers now as he rubs himself against me.

Dallas looks at me as he grabs my hips, pressing himself against me, claiming my mouth in his. The feeling of his tongue sends shivers down my spine.

I can taste myself on him.

I never promised to keep his clothes on.

Fingers hook into his waistband, pulling it down, freeing him from his confinement. My heart rate is working overtime.

He's breathing in my oxygen as I exhale. I breathe him in when he exhales. His back flexes with each movement, and my hands roam everywhere.

His boxers are completely off. He's just outside my parted thighs. Gliding back and forth between my folds, it's slick with my excitement, and he's hard with his.

I catch his eyes with mine as we kiss, and my hand moves down his torso to his manhood. Going in between our legs, I try to grip around his girth firmly. My teeth bite into my lower lip, drawing just a trace of blood that I love. I can smell him getting more and more aroused, and it drives me to continue on.

His breathing grows more intense as I work him up and down. My thumb glides over the tip, and his moistness starts to leak out. His eyes close with a moan. He lifts himself over the top of me, muscles in his arms hard with the strain of holding himself up. I bite into his bicep, and another hard moan tumbles from this male's throat.

His reaction to my touch encourages me that I am doing something right.

"Lay on your back." A whispered command in his ear has him doing what I say now.

Straddling his lower legs, I watch his eyes traveling over my chest, down my belly, looking between my legs…that the torn material is showing exactly what I have.

Nothing is left to the imagination.

"Rya." My name slips from his open mouth. It's deeper than he usually speaks. More of a voice that others don't get to hear.

Looking at him, my eyes memorize every inch of

him. My hand keeps its motion of up and down. I can feel his contour, exploring the skin with my closed palm. He gasps, grabbing onto my outer thighs with claws that hook into my skin. I want more from this male beneath me.

A hard moan escapes from deep within his chest, and my insides start to quiver with the music he's making. My curves press against muscles as I bend my head down, tracing him with my tongue. I'm tasting the tip of him. His essence is now on my taste buds; it's salty, like nothing I have tasted before. He's pulsating in my hand as my mouth closes around him.

Taking him into my mouth, I let my tongue explore his ridge, sucking him up and down, letting teeth gently brush against sensitive skin.

His body reacts, muscles contracting and relaxing, growling deep his appreciation of what I am doing to him. My ears perk up with how I can make him feel and sound.

Gripping him firmly at the base, I twirl my tongue around him, exploring what I have never had before in my mouth. I think I give a gasp as I feel him pulse inside himself and groan out loud.

The way I'm making him feel is addicting. I can live off this feeling, providing such pleasure for someone.

His hips lift slightly as my mouth goes down on him, hands in my hair. His hips withdraw himself from me only to push back in. Cheeks suck in, creating a suction tight and moist.

He's looking at me the whole time, eyes wide, breathing shallow. It feels as if the energy around him is growing, getting sucked from the room and into him. What does he think as he's watching me please him with my mouth?

I let my tongue slide from the base to the tip while I watch him watch me. My teeth have slightly descended; I can see him looking at them as his start to make an appearance. His thighs are quivering now as he starts to thrust himself into my open mouth. His hand wraps into my hair, guiding me at his pace.

With a quick movement, I'm pinned underneath him, and his teeth are at my neck. His hand replaces mine. He's at my entrance, holding himself there still as a statue, teeth extended, holding me to him. He pushes very slightly inside me, so just the very tip rests at my entrance. He trembles his release, shuddering explosively inside, coating me with his scent.

The very essence of who he is.

Dallas's fluid fills my insides up, leaking down my bare thighs, creating a wet spot on the sheets.

"Rya, don't move." His voice is hard against my neck, his canines dimpling my skin, but not puncturing through. He could mark me now if he wanted to; I would be so easy to take.

A groan from him has another fresh wave saturating my insides.

His whole body is tense and rippling with his pleasure. We stay like this for a minute, breathing hard, while he gains control of himself.

Dallas rolls to his side, bringing me with him, pressed against his chest.

"I almost marked you, Rya. I almost lost my

control." Pressing his lips to the top of my head, my cheek is flush with his chest. My fingers trace the flesh of his back.

How would I feel if he marked me? I'm conflicted. My wolf is full steam ahead; he's a quality male. He is a provider of meat, very simple in her eyes. He's already her male, no matter what the skin side thinks.

"I think we need to talk about this." He grabs the back of my hair, pulling my head back so he can look into my eyes.

"I can feel your hesitance, Rya." A shadow passes over his turquoise eyes. I love that color; it's the only color of jewelry I wear. It compliments my eyes, so I've been told.

"It's a big step for me, Dallas." This has to be as truthful as possible; I could never lie to him no matter how hard truth hurts.

"I understand, Rya. It's a big step. I just want you to know that I am having a hard time refraining from claiming you. I'm not sure what will happen with my mark on your neck, but inside I already feel as if you're mine. I have been given a second chance, and I don't want to waste this chance."

"I'm scared, Dallas. I'm afraid. I don't know what to expect with all this. I feel a great attraction to you, my wolf has marked you as mine, but at the same time, I have this connection with Clayton that can't be denied. I know he doesn't want me. I know this in my brain. In my body, I feel him so deeply it consumes me when I'm near him. Yet at the same time, I can feel you inside me, not as powerful, but I feel your presence as well." I look at his hurt eyes,

249

his clenched jaw, his pain seeping out.

"I understand, Rya. I know the pull you feel. I understand how consuming it is. I'll fight for you. I will fight for the right to be your number one choice. I just need a chance to prove I can be that male for you." His phone starts ringing, in his pants on my bedroom floor.

Leaning over me, he answers it.

"Aurora, what's the matter?" He closes his eyes for a brief second. "I'm coming." Getting off me, he pulls up his boxers.

"It seems Cash is going to kill Clayton. Aurora is doing her best to keep him out, but Cash is very persistent." His voice is filled with annoyance.

Getting up, I change quickly. I need to see this for myself. We walk outside to the car. The sky looks washed out in grey. Maybe rain is coming, or maybe the first real snow. It's crisp enough outside for that to happen.

Pulling into the clinic parking lot, I see Kennedy sitting on the steps with her head in her hands, rocking back and forth crying. Cash is ramming the door open with his body, Aurora on the other side, using her body to block his path in. That big metal door is caving in with the power of his shoulder.

Kennedy's head angles up. She slowly stands, looking at me with death—not hatred, but with someone wanting to kill someone else.

"Sit down!" Dallas's authority has her stiffen. Slowly, she slinks back down into the same position she was in before. Her shoulders are tucked in slightly, head bowed.

"Cash!" One word spoken in dominance makes

Cash stop his next rush to the door.

Cash's turbulent eyes regard Dallas.

Dallas regards Cash's vicious violence by sneering his teeth at his brother.

"What did I tell you, Cash?" Dallas takes a step toward his brother. Cash looks wild, feral to a certain degree as he angles his body to face his brother's full wrath head on.

"I'm going to kill that wolf."

"No, you're not. He's not yours to kill." Kennedy's tear-streaked face looks up toward Dallas, understanding crossing her face. She begins to stand up.

"Sit down." The quiet savageness from Dallas has Kennedy sitting still as a statue, not moving.

Dallas snaps viciously toward Cash. The Alpha in Dallas is making my wolf uncontrollable. She's trying to claw and scratch her way out to stand on his right with her back straight to give support to her male.

"Rya, control yourself." His voice pounds into my chest, making my fierce wolf whimper slightly.

"Cash, stop now!" he roars. The few birds that stay for the winter have now taken to flight.

Cash stills, shaking in his skin. I can see the way he tries to resist his brother's voice, but he is no match for Dallas.

"Cash, I thought I made a good choice when I asked you to be my Beta. Don't make me regret that decision." Dallas gives him a calm but murderous glare.

"What happened?" Cash staggers back slightly.

"She wouldn't let me in." He points his finger at

the door.

"Kennedy just keeps telling me how I won't be enough for her." He pounds his fist against the clinic door over and over again. His knuckles bleed, dripping on the steps that greet our patients. The effort he's putting into her is commendable, but when do you decide you put your all into things or maybe it's time just to walk away?

"I'll take her to talk with him. Cash, you stay out here. Rya, come with us." Cash sits on the step in defeat. "Aurora, open the door." A click of locks tells us we're free to walk in.

He has Kennedy stand in front of him while I follow behind. My wolf wants to meet her wolf.

"Rya, stop it!" Dallas turns his face toward me, eyes blazing. My wolf whimpers and crawls down on her belly with her tail wrapped around her body.

When we enter his healing room, it's dark. The window shades are drawn closed, only allowing just the faintest stream of grey light in.

"You shouldn't be here." His voice is tight with emotion.

"Kennedy wants to talk with you." Dallas betrays no emotion while speaking to Clayton.

"What is it that you need, Kennedy?" Clayton's voice doesn't hold any softness in it, more annoyance than anything else. His white bandages are still seeping red from blood that doesn't want to stop oozing out his skin.

Kennedy looks taken aback by his tone.

"I just—"

"Kennedy, you have a mate. You need to be with him. My wolf will tear you apart if it gets a chance.

I can't risk that. I need for you to be with him, give him a chance. He's a good wolf, Kennedy. I'm not for you. I was never yours to begin with. I love you with my soul, but I'm not yours. I don't want you coming back here. I don't want to see your face again, do you understand?" His voice holds nothing, just indifference toward her.

"You don't mean that." Her voice quivers low and soft. Can she feel the knife entering her skin the way I did? Can she feel it slice her open, choking her breath on the pain? I hope she feels it. I hope her whole body doubles over. I want to put my own knife into her back.

"I do. Now go." He turns away from us. His hands are still tied above his head this time; they must rotate positions.

"You could just kill him, Clay. He's no match for you," she pleads.

"He's not the wolf I want to kill, Kennedy." Clayton's eyes find Dallas's. Kennedy's hand comes up over her mouth, a muffled cry pouring from the cracks between her fingers. I see Clayton's muscles tensing up, and a groan escapes his mouth that's full of pain. She's feeling those knives now. Hopefully, they are serrated slightly, not a smooth blade.

The look of hurt and shock on her face makes my laughter want to bubble up out of my throat.

"Do you like this, Rya? You find this funny?" Clayton's voice is muffled into his pillow. "You like it when other wolves hurt?"

"No," I breathe out.

"Rya, let's be perfectly clear. I don't want you.

My wolf does. He's going to fight for you, but me, I want nothing to do with you. I could just do you, but it seems that someone else already is. So you really have nothing to offer me that's worth anything." His tight tone makes my skin crawl. This is who I was having doubts over.

"You're just a weak little wolf who revels in the misery of others." Clayton lets his voice stab me from the outside. He thinks that I'm that type of wolf.

Dallas sits on the chair next to the bed, pulling it close so his knees touch the mattress. He leans down so his elbows are touching his knees. His mouth is very close to Clayton's face. I can see Clayton smelling the air, his mouth pulling back in a snarl.

"You should kill me now while you have a chance before I come for you." Clayton's voice is smooth as silk with a touch of violence.

Dallas smiles at him like he's a small pup with big dreams.

CHAPTER 22

Eat

Posturing without speaking, these two males regard each other, neither looking away. Eyes convey messages of war that no words could ever do justice for.

A smile shows teeth from Dallas he won't use yet, and Clayton's sneer reveals teeth he can't use yet.

"Kenny!" Kimberly's juvenile voice is at the entrance of the clinic.

"Cover me up." Clayton shifts from menace to concern, almost a pleading quality in that voice of his. Kennedy goes to him, bringing the sheet over his back up to his neck. He gives a small hiss of pain from the contact of the covers. She touches his hair, feeling the side of his jaw in careless movements, and I wonder if the stubble is prickly on her flesh.

A flash of white, sharp teeth almost bites her fingers off. His wolf might not be able to ascend

255

yet, but a very small part has just shown Kennedy what it wants to do to her. He wants to eat the hand that was just touching his face.

"Stay away from me!" His jaw muscles twitch with the effort of trying to stay clenched.

Her face shows her struggle. She looks down at her finger. A very small cut is noticeable on her hand.

Love bites. She needs to be careful or else her body will be scarred with that kind of love.

Will she put in the effort it will take to convince his wolf that she's the one for him? Will she quit on their love?

"Kenny!" Kimberly runs into her brother's healing room and into Kennedy's arms, pressing her nose into her neck. "I've missed you so much." They are holding each other so close. Kennedy is stroking her hair now, soothing this small pregnant female's emotions.

Cash leans against the door frame, eyes only for Clayton.

"Stop now!" Dallas's voice is even with no inflection in tone, meant to be listened to. Cash straightens slightly, looking at Kennedy.

"You promised me, Kenny. You promised to help me if this happened. I need you." All of our heads tilt slightly at this young female's words.

"What did she promise to help you with?" Clayton's eyes are on Kennedy, yet he asked Kimberly the question.

A peculiar feeling starts to crawl underneath my skin, prickling down my spine.

"She told me she would treat my pup like her

own. That you and she would raise it like your own. I didn't have to worry about anything." Hidden truths are revealed.

Disgust rolls through me. Kennedy was willing to risk the death of Kimberly, her lover's sister. She was willing to possibly sacrifice a life so she could raise a life as her own.

Truth can be disgusting sometimes, all in the name of love.

"What did you do?" Clayton's eyes now really look at Kennedy, seeing her without the glamour that blurred her lines to him. He's seeing the naked truth in all its repulsive glory. You can tell he's thinking this by the way his mouth is turned down, his sourness filling the room now, making me start to breathe through my mouth.

"I never did anything." She can't meet his eyes, a lie from those vocal cords that shake slightly.

"What did you do?" he repeats

Her guilty eyes dart around the room, while she still holds Kimberly to her chest. Cash straightens up, looking at her with disgust. A growl escapes his throat, fist clenched at this side.

"Tell him!" Cash is red-faced, steaming mad. I eye him up and down, still wondering when he will quit, what his breaking point is, what it will take for him to throw away what the moon so graciously gave him? He's leaning up against the wall, as if he needs it to keep himself standing. Does this new light in her character make his knees weak, just not in a good way?

Her sharp eyes flash to Cash. She can't hide her disgust for this male who's supposed to be her biggest treasure.

"You unlocked the door, didn't you? It was you!" The light switch must be turning on in his brain, putting everything together. His eyes travel up and down his everything, looking at her in disbelief.

What's more hurtful...the lie that she's been hiding, or the fact that she put his sister's life at risk for their love?

"Let me explain." Now she turns to plead with a lover who doesn't want to hear anything her tarnished mouth has to say. Tears leak down her reddened cheeks, and a sob escapes her lips as she tries to get the words out. She shakes her head to him. He looks like he's lost that loving feeling for her.

His hands turning to fists, he pulls on the chains that are attached to the bed holding him in his place.

Her words are thick like molasses trying to go down a metal drain, slow and copious, as if she's trying to find the right lies to spew. Except we all can see the lie that's standing stagnant and rotten in the air.

Dallas looks at her in such disgust it's hard not to flinch away. Great rolling waves of rage for that female is lighting a fire inside him. I can see a tremor in his hand as he pushes himself away from Clayton's bed. He takes a step toward the two females who are still holding each other. A growl roars out of the base of his chest that has us all shaking except Clayton; he's trying his best to get out of those leather cuffs that hold him to the bed.

The situation is quickly declining, spiraling

downward as the new Alpha snaps teeth toward a female who's without honor in his mind. Such gripping feelings of emotion are threatening to overtake him.

I can actually feel my insides darken with his need to end a wolf who is tainted with an incurable sickness.

Clayton is pulling with more strength, the steel bed shaking and rattling with the force of him trying to get free of his jailer's cuffs.

His body trembles as his legs try to bend into a kneeling position. He just can't do it as he falls against the mattress over and over again, not giving up until dark crimson blood saturates the last spot of white on those bandages.

He's grunting through clenched teeth, trying to get out of his confinement. He screams as soon as he accidentally flips over onto his back. The cover falls on the floor. I see my mate for the first time naked. I can't look away from the sight before me. Dallas growls low in his chest as my eyes try to divert themselves from something I have imagined for such a long time.

Another scream echoes in the small room. He's having a hard time breathing, trying to catch his breath, trying to flip himself back over. Dallas calmly stands to place a hand carefully underneath his hip to flip him back on his stomach. He pulls his covers back over his naked backside.

Kimberly's screams match Clayton's as he tries to muffle them with the pillow.

Kennedy's legs give out, tumbling her to the ground hard. She's crawling toward him, begging him for understanding, a chance to explain her actions. Crying on hands and knees. Pleading with her unbearable heart pain. He doesn't answer her back. He shakes his head, yelling for everyone to get out.

He's no longer pulling on the restraints. He looks immobilized with pain. I wonder if it's physical or heartfelt that he's feeling?

Dallas now goes to a drawer and pulls out a syringe and a glass vial. He cracks the lid open, putting the needle in and sucking out the clear liquid. Walking toward Clayton, he injects him in the shoulder, plunging its contents in his muscle.

Kimberly's looking at Kennedy now, who's on the floor. Her emotions are vomiting out for all to see.

"You left the door open." Disbelief is so concentrated in a soft whisper that I can hardly hear it. I watch as this small juvenile pulls her arm up and punches her in the face, busting her nose wide open. Cash is on Kimberly instantly, picking her up. Clayton is trying to combat whatever Dallas has put into his system, but he's no match for those drugs.

I take a step toward Cash, who has this little one in his arms, and my own darkness takes me over. A protection I have never felt before surges into my system. Dallas is on Cash faster than I can get to him. Picking him up by the scruff of his neck, he walks him out of the healing room.

"Get up!" I command Kennedy, whose hand is trying to stop the flow of blood.

"Make me." Her words are flung right back in my face.

Dallas comes back, picks Kennedy up by the scruff of her neck. His claws are out, puncturing her flesh very slightly. He's holding his great anger back, trying to contain what his nature wants him to do: end her quickly without regret.

Going over to Kimberly, I walk her out of the room as Clayton closes his eyes, not able to open them back up again.

He's going to have so much time thinking about all the truths he learned today.

Walking out into the parking lot with Kimberly, I watch the grey sky shed the first flurries of fall, shimmying down from the sky in their winter waltz. Two flakes of snow land on each hand. They say no two snowflakes are alike. I feel both tingle my skin, only to melt and disappear at the same time like they were never really there in the first place.

Luna Grace is standing next to Cash, whispering something in his ear. He just shakes his head no. Dallas has his arms crossed over his chest as if he's restraining himself from Kennedy.

Her posture is straight back defiance, meeting the eyes of all the wolves who are circling around her.

"Do it!" she spits out to Cash. "You can't. You know why you can't?" She tilts her head toward her mate with a sick smile on her face.

"Because you're a weak little wolf." Luna Grace is on her instantly. It looks so easy the way her hand wraps around Kennedy's throat, lifting her whole body up in the air before slamming her hard against the ground, where the wind is knocked out of her lungs.

Teeth bared in a feral grin, Luna Grace allows Kennedy to see what she possesses.

"I have raised Cash since he was a small thought in my belly. I will not tolerate any more of your words against him. I don't care when you are alone and fling those words in the privacy of your own home, but when I am around, I will not stand for it." I watch the way her hand wraps around her ruined throat, squeezing tightly.

"He's my male. He has the biggest heart out of all my males. He's my beautiful savage, he's hurting, but you just can't see this, can you? I have never met a female like you before, and I hope to the moon I never meet one again. I have raised him well. He is far from weak. If he were as weak as you say, your throat would already be opened up a long time ago. He's giving you a chance. You're just too stupid to see it." Serpentine black eyes regard Kennedy. Her focus is vicious and cunning. I feel as if the Luna has taken off her mask, unveiling her true dislike for this female for everyone to see.

"I will show Cash how much a mother can love her young and end you. Is that what you want? A mother's hard love?" Both of them are frozen in their spots. Kennedy, unable to hold her eyes any longer, looks away in defeat. Her whole body wilts on itself.

Cash just looks away as Kennedy gets up by herself, no one offering a hand to help her.

Kimberly whimpers quietly to herself.

I walk toward her with my arms extended, as if going to bring her into my chest, but she steps back, looking at me as if I'm crazy.

"This is all your fault. If you didn't come back, none of this would have happened. My parents would still be here, and everything would be just how it was!" Her full rage is directed at me.

"They wanted me back, Kimberly. They called me back. Do you think I wanted to come back? It's easy to point a finger at me, but in truth, I'm not the cause of all this." I try to be as gentle with her as I can. She's young, pregnant, with emotions on a roller coaster ride that's probably hard to control.

"Maybe if you weren't such a quitter." His voice scrapes against my skin. I feel sorry for him and hate him at the same time as my eyes meet Cash head on in a collision of violence.

He runs hard at me, only to be knocked down by Dallas.

"Enough, Cash! You're relieved of your duties. You need to go back home until you can control yourself more. Even then, I don't know if you're the right wolf for the Beta position. Caleb, you're here until things settle down." Dallas looks at his father for the okay.

"Caleb is needed back at home. He has to get ready for the trials, unless you've had a change of heart?" Luna Grace angles her hopeful eyes toward her oldest son. His father waits for a reply.

Dallas turns to me, looking in contemplation. Big breath in and he releases it out.

He's at my side, hands on my shoulders.

"Do you trust me?" Our eyes are connected, and I swear his are getting lighter, like my own. It's unnerving.

Do I trust this wolf? He has never lied to me so

far. He has always told me the truth.

"Yes."

"I want you to go with my father. I want you to visit my home pack, see where I come from, have my father train you. It won't be easy. You're going to learn about me, about yourself, things you might not like. I'm going to take a chance, Rya, on us, and let you go for a while so you can learn how to be a wolf and lead by my side, if that's what you want." He's holding onto my shoulders hard, as if he doesn't really want to let them go.

All his brothers are looking at him now with smiles on their faces.

"I'll take care of everything here. Your females will be taken care of. I promise you this, they will not be neglected, even though I hate it. I will do it for you, for us." His mother has her hand on her mouth, a tear sliding down her face of what only can be described as happiness slips out.

"Little Moon, it's very simple. All you need to do is eat." The Silverback Alpha's deep voice bellows out as Dallas's face pales slightly with a look of fear.

CHAPTER 23

Name

Silence can fill a space, its tension wrapping around everyone like a humid summer day, oppressive and smothering as you breathe in the air. It's how I feel sitting in the back of the vehicle with Dallas's family. I don't think they like the company they are bringing back to their home.

Kennedy had fought to her last breath not wanting to come, kicking and screaming, until that Silverback male uttered just one word into her ear...*stop*.

She hasn't said one word since. Maybe she's resigned to her fate.

I get an unobstructed view of the side of her face when she watches the land pass by in a blur from the window. I'm directly behind her. Watching her shell just breathe.

Her fading highlighted hair looks somewhat dry and limp, her curls not as bouncy. Her face is blemish-free, and even without the illusion of

265

makeup she still is beautiful. High cheekbones, thick full mouth, long black lashes that curl naturally. Her clothes are all rumpled up; they don't smell too fresh. I'm not even sure if they are her own clothes by the way they fit her.

Sometimes her head angles to the side so her eye glares at me before looking out the window again. I know she can feel me staring at her. I can't look away, so I just stare at the back of her head.

Cash doesn't say a word to me. His head is turned away in his own little purgatory. He pretends to focus his concentration on what's outside the car window, but I bet all he can think about are what truths he's learned.

I want to scream in his face, to keep putting that effort in, don't quit now, big guy. Show me what strength you have inside to fight for what's yours.

Instead, I just let the silence hang outside my mouth, not saying a word.

I can see some of Cash's brothers looking at him in pity. He doesn't deserve this. I can see sharp teeth lift ever so slightly toward Kennedy. Can she feel all those teeth around her from every direction?

When we stop to eat, I'm placed right beside Luna Grace on her left. Cash is on his father's left, so that means I had to sit directly across from Kennedy. She keeps her eyes diverted the whole time. I don't think she really wants to eat, but that body of hers is just beginning with its ultimate betrayal.

Her heat makes it impossible not to eat as it starts to prepare itself for a future. She eats everything on her plate and finishes off Cash's food as well.

He didn't feed her from his hand, but he did offer her what was left over. Her heat will be in full swing soon, her body packing away the extra calories that are needed to nurture and sustain a future life.

The Luna looks at Kennedy's empty plates with a knowing look.

"Are you still hungry, Kennedy?" Her words are spoken without violence this time.

"Yes," she answers truthfully. Is this the first truth she has told these wolves?

She looks at all the plates on the table still having some food on them. It's the Alpha who breaks his sandwich in half, handing it to Cash, only for him to put it on her plate. The rest of the brothers follow, their posture not comfortable with what they are doing, but they follow their father's example.

The Luna puts some of her meal on her plate as well. I'm the only one who hasn't contributed. I'm holding in my hand what I was saving for last.

It's the first thing I smelled when I entered this restaurant, fresh handmade rolls. Whoever made it added raisins and walnuts while kneading the dough. Sugar sprinkles the top with a small dusting of cinnamon.

No one is looking at me, but they're all watching in their own way. I take a deep breath. I have to imagine this as feeding the potential life she might host inside herself and not really feeding her. With one more smell of the roll, I place it on her plate. My jaw clenches tight as I look at my own empty plate.

I'm still hungry, except I have no future my body is preparing for.

Cash's eyes lift to mine in surprise before he gets up, walking away from the table and out the door, letting it close gently behind him.

Kennedy begins to eat everything else that's on her plate, the hormones of her heat driving her to consume as much as possible.

She doesn't say a word of thanks; she just eats what's offered to her.

Luna Grace has a smile on her face, watching her devour the food in greed.

"I remember my heats. I couldn't get enough food or you in me." She turns sultry eyes to her male. Her sons start to pretend to gag at the table, looking uncomfortable, while Alpha Clinton grabs her hand in his big mitts. He brings her fingertips to his smiling mouth, kissing them.

"We're right here, sitting right here." Carson wipes his napkin over his mouth, spitting the last of his food in it before getting up and joining Cash outside. The rest of her males just shake their heads at them.

"Rya, when can we expect your heat to come?" If I had food in my mouth, I would have choked, spitting the contents out on the table. The two remaining males' chairs scrape against the tile floor as they push them away in absolute disgust. They make their way outside, leaving the four of us alone together. Kennedy continues to shove food in her face while I pale.

"I've never had one." Best to be truthful. Why lie

now?

"You're sterile?" Alpha Clinton words tumble out, while Kennedy actually looks at me in open-mouthed shock, to the point I can see her chewed-up food.

"Impossible. You smell fertile, almost as if you are always just beginning your heat," Luna Grace confesses.

"I never went through one." My head hangs shamefully. This is my secret no one has ever known until now. I should have told Dallas about this before I left, but there was no time to talk before I decided to go away with his family.

Kennedy's full attention is on the conversation as she takes the first bite of that bun I gave her. I can see how it must have hit her taste buds the way she savors the flavor of it.

An image flashes in my brain of me snatching the bun back and shoving it in my mouth, eating the rest of it. I don't act on that thought; I have to put my hands underneath my thighs, locking them in place.

"I'm going to wait outside with our males." Alpha Clinton just throws some money on the table, more than enough to cover everything as he walks away.

"You're just a late bloomer, Rya. I think that once my son marks you that you will experience your first heat." She says these words, but I can't believe what she says.

"Maybe." One word was spoken to the Luna that conveys my doubt.

Kennedy finally finishes everything. I notice her

undoing the top button of her pants that are cutting into the smooth skin of her belly. She keeps her head down as she makes her way outside to the waiting vehicle, the Luna in between us as we walk.

This is the longest ride I have ever taken, the landscape changing now. Instead of the great sentinel pines with whispering willow trees that I'm used to, a northern forest starts to take hold, tall pines, firs, hemlocks, and spruces littering the land we are driving in.

Pulling onto a dirt road off the main highway, we come to a ridge looking down the steep slope. We get to take in the grand expanse of nature that humbles my soul. Even Kennedy's eyes are taking all this in. The wind up here hurtles itself against the vehicle, making it swerve slightly with each gust. I think a storm is going to hit very soon.

Firs are packed so densely together that all you can see down below is a canopy of green tipped in white.

Another hour on this road has small houses tucked into the forest's edge, with a lake behind them. They look like summer cottages, but smoke is coming out of all the chimneys, saying this is all year-round living.

I can't help but look outside and take everything in. I have only been out of my pack to train, and even then I was really not allowed to explore on my own.

We pull up to a moderate-sized home. It has a windmill, and solar panels on the roof, fully self-sufficient.

All the males get out of the car as one. They go

270

to the back and pull bags out, loading them up their arms.

Cash sticks close to his baggage, pulling Kennedy along by the wrist.

She doesn't try to pull away from his grasp, and I can actually see the small shiver that affects her skin. I wonder if Clayton ever made her skin shiver like that. I'm sure he made her legs quiver, but did he ever shiver her skin with just a touch?

Walking inside a mud room, I see coats and robes hung along one wall with boots lining the ground. I follow behind everyone, and we come into a very large kitchen. It's what I dream about the way old fashion mixes with just a touch of modern. It's clean and full of the smells of homemade love.

"Cash, do you want the spare room for Kennedy?" Like it's his decision where she sleeps. She doesn't look at him. Instead, her head is bowed, looking at the tile floor, very docile.

"She can have the spare room." I can see the relief uncoil the tension in her shoulders.

"Rya, that means you can have my son's room. It's his juvenile room. It really hasn't been changed since he had his own house built." Giving a slight smile, I'm somewhat apprehensive to intrude on his space.

Before I left, he asked me to go through all his things, look through every drawer, every nook, even under his mattress. He told me he had a home there that the pack got together and built them. He hasn't stepped foot in it since her death. He encouraged me to go through everything, and when I find something that is hard for me to understand to call

271

him about it and we'll discuss it. I still have to tell him about me and everything that I haven't gotten a chance to inform him about.

I walk through the living room. It's an eclectic blend of furniture, nothing matching, but everything working well together.

"This is beautiful." My voice is soft as I run my fingertips along the wooden cabinet that holds a china doll collection. Even Kennedy comes over to admire the piece before us.

"My mate found that old piece of wood at the dump. She had me bring it back here, and she fixed up, and now it's the most beautiful piece of furniture we own. She's really good at repairing broken and thrown away things. As long as the core isn't rotten, she can fix anything. You wouldn't believe what that looked like before she got her hands on it. Took her awhile, she put in a lot of effort and time in, but in the end, it turned out beautiful." He wraps his arms around his mate, kissing her neck. They have perfect symmetry.

Their love seems so easy.

"Kennedy, we expect certain thing out of you, and one of those things is respect. If you respect the rules here, we should have no problems." That Silverback male's eyes warn her not to step out of line.

"Little moon, I'm coming for you early in the morning. Please be ready." My eyes find his again. I just can't help but try and stare him down.

Something deep within me wants to be his master.

He doesn't look away. Instead, he takes the first

step toward me, those eyes pinning me in my place. "I'm going to teach you how to back that up." His hands go over my eyes, closing them for me.

"If you look at me that way again, I'm going to have to put you down hard." I think I'm in over my head as I watch his massive body walk away from me, taking his female by the hand.

"Come on, I'll take you upstairs to his room." Carson tugs on my arm, so I follow him. Kennedy and Cash are already ahead of me on the steps.

"This is his room." A giant number one painted in white is on the door. In the paint, I also notice the awful curses written inside the number.

"We didn't like how he put that number up outside his room, so we let him know what we thought of him." Carson smiles with the memories.

I can't help but laugh at all the funny things they wrote to him, brothers and their unique way of communicating love.

My eyes fall again to all the name calling, but then I notice the I love you, the get better, the I'm here for you, brother, we love her. This must have been written after the death of his mate. It almost makes my eyes water seeing this in a good way, in a way that they care about him.

My attention swings to the door beside Dallas's room as Cash leans in toward Kennedy with a sinister stare.

"Remember, Kennedy, if you try to run, this is my land, and I know every inch of it. I will find you, bring you back, and collar you until you won't remember who you are." A look of horror crosses her face. I believe in my soul he will do it if she gets out of line; he's that type of wolf.

She quickly glides past him before closing the door behind her quietly. He just stands there, inhaling, as his forehead goes against the wooden door frame.

Their canvas is bruised and torn at the edges, splitting down the middle. His face shows his sorrow and misery. He runs his fingers through his hair that's just starting to grow out from being shaved regularly. His eyes turn to mine. I've been caught gawking. His layers exposed, his gaze burns into mine. He looks so defeated before turning away from me and entering his own room for the night.

Entering Dallas's room, I take a big breath as pictures of his youth smile back at me. His brothers from all sorts of ages, his friends, her, they all stare back at me with stories to tell.

Putting my bag on the bed, I sit on the edge while looking around.

It's a big room with an attached bathroom. It really doesn't smell like him; his scent is stale, only barely clinging inside this space that was once his own.

Letters on his desk catch my eye. They look like they have been crumpled up at some time, only to be smoothed out again in reverence.

I lean over and pick one up. It's addressed to Clayton Dallas Valentine, his acceptance letter to medical school. I drop the letter, and it floats down like a feather drifting from side to side as it lands gracefully at my feet.

Pulling out my phone, I place my first call to him.

He picks up, not letting it ring twice.

"What's your first name?" My voice feels different, like someone else is saying these words.

He responds instantly.

"*Clayton.*"

I need to sit down. His mattress is firm without a lot of give. Hanging up on him, I toss the phone away.

Let my pain begin.

Acknowledgements

First, I have to start off by thanking my family—Scott, Hailee, and Phoenix—for your incredible understanding of time. Thank you for letting me be engrossed in the world of the Valentines.

I need to thank Naoures, Monica, Ethel, Portia, Sarah, Farah, Micha (Sarah), Lidia, and Petra, for holding my hand when I needed it the most. Your encouragement have brought me here today.

About the Author

Rachelle Mills lives in Canada with her family and two dogs. She's a lover of all things that have to do with Nature and Wildlife.

Mills has won acclaim from readers for her fantastically realized paranormal werewolf universes, where alpha males fight tooth and claw and society – more often than not – is determined to make the path of true love as rocky and uncomfortable as possible.

Her rich, paranormal universe is packed with characters that frustrate and enthrall readers with an expert grasp of the complexities of the primal fight that werewolves have; their human, controlled side, and the vicious, ugly, and virtually untamable were-side which can leave a trail of destruction in its wake.

Mills' writing style is charged with emotion and richly descriptive, bringing the universe of her often-gritty stories into vivid life.

Facebook:
https://www.facebook.com/Rachelle-Mills-298700590732805/?ref=bookmarks

Twitter:
https://twitter.com/whiskeyqueenn?lang=en

Goodreads:
https://www.goodreads.com/author/show/14827762.Rachelle_Mills

Instagram:
https://www.instagram.com/whiskeyqueenn/

Join our Reader Group on Facebook and don't miss out on meeting our authors and entering epic giveaways!

Limitless Reading

Where reading a book
is your first step to becoming
limitless...

LIMITLESS PUBLISHING *Reader Group*

Join today! *"Where reading a book is your first step to becoming limitless..."*

https://www.facebook.com/groups/Limitless Reading/